GEIST FLEISCH

By Christian Baines

GEIST FLEISCH

Acknowledgements

Thank you to all who've stared into the gaping maw of Queer horror and speculative fiction and said "more please." We have always been here, and you keep us here. Thank you!

Thank you to all my co-con-spirit-ors of the Haunted Hearts series for your encouragement, signal-boosting, inspiration, feedback, and determination to get our strange little collection out into the world.

Thanks to A J Dolman, Ryan Lawrence and Blake Allwood for your feedback and encouragement through early drafts of the book. Thanks to friends in Berlin who kept me coming back and wanting more (thankfully in a more cheerful period than Callum's), and to Isherwood (and Kander and Ebb) for lighting that first spark of fascination.

Thanks to the many friends, close family, and readers who've cheered me on, come to signings or launches, or just let me rave about whatever idea has got me excited in that moment.

I am deeply privileged to have you all.

CHAPTER ONE

"Come on! You promised you'd keep up!"

Callum narrowly dodged a collision with a well-dressed couple with a well-timed leap left. He followed Anne's blue hat as it bobbed up and down through the crowd now spilling from the Metropol onto the rainy street near Nollendorfplatz. All he knew about the bars in this district was that the richer nancies favoured them, at least on those nights they decided to give the rough-trade boys of Kreuzberg a rest. He knew this mostly from the boastings of Viktor, who lodged in the apartment above his own in Neukölln. The number of furtive-looking gentlemen Callum had spied climbing the stairs to Viktor's told him enough about how Viktor supplemented the meagre wages granted a machine worker. He'd tried to take it in good humour when Viktor had suggested using his own physical assets to top up his wallet, though of course the German hadn't been joking. Perhaps he'd meant it as a compliment, or a come-on. Callum had always been lousy at reading other fellows' intentions, even without a language barrier.

"No, no, it's this way!"

"I thought we were going to the Eldorado?" Callum had heard stories of Berlin's most infamous nightclub and cabaret. He'd arrived too late to see Dietrich there, of course. So had Anne, in spite of the fanciful story she'd concocted in a letter that had outraged her father, sent her mother sick to bed with worry, and convinced Callum that Berlin, with its unchallenged freedom, sounded far more exciting than dreary, rainy, dirty Nottingham. He'd just as soon convinced himself that the adventure it promised would not be obstructed by little obstacles such as not understanding German.

"We are, later! I promised someone a drink first."

"You promised *me* a drink," he reminded her, darting between a cab pulling into the curb and a plump woman wrapped in furs. The fur-laden *Frau* glared at them with indignation as Anne shot off down Kleiststrasse, a busy street that ran parallel to the U-Bahn.

The rain grew heavier, and Callum quickened his pace just enough to see Anne disappear inside a small, darkened doorway. Had he paid less attention, he might not have seen her at all.

"*Guten Abend,*" Anne greeted the plump, somewhat gruff looking woman guarding the entrance with all the ferocity of Cerberus protecting the Underworld. Anne shucked off her wet coat and made a show of shaking it off onto the street. The human hell hound accepted it with precisely the kind of small snort Callum had thought she'd make and acquiesced. That was, until she saw him. Anne, it seemed, was ready for that too, firing off a cheerful string of German that Callum couldn't hope to keep up with. It didn't buy them a smile, but it was enough to admit Callum's sodden coat with a tired sigh.

As he followed Anne to the bar, through the smoky atmosphere of the tiny club, Callum looked around at the women surrounding them. Many sat in pairs at intimate tables. At least three affected sharp suits, cigarettes glowing in the darkness as they animated themselves in conversation. The bartender at least greeted Anne with a smile, and Callum recognised the word *Freundin*. It most decidedly had not been directed at him. Anne's arm linked around his, continuing the exchange with intimidating fluency until the bartender too, acquiesced. Callum didn't need to understand the words to know he was the bone of contention.

"It's all right, darling," Anne assured him. "We'll have one drink here then move on, all right?"

"If you're sure," he muttered, now more than certain he was not the bar's preferred clientele.

"*Liebchen!*" The warm, rich voice belonged to a woman who put a gentle hand on Anne's shoulder before exchanging kisses with her.

"Helene, I want you to meet my cousin… Well, not my actual cousin, but we've known each other for simply donkey's years and—"

"Callum," he said, extending a hand he hoped would dispel Helene's bafflement.

"Pleased to meet you," the woman answered, somewhat stiffly. "*Entscheuldegung, aber*… Anne has… help me with English, but…"

"That's more English than I know German," he answered with a laugh that wasn't returned.

"Drink?" Helene asked Anne.

Callum wondered if this offer extended to him as Anne rattled off some order he didn't recognise. Seeing how she looked at Helene, along with the two drinks the bartender slid to the women, he quickly realised it didn't.

"*Drink?*" the bartender asked him. It felt like an act of rescue.

"Uh… *ja. Ein Bier?*" His affectation made Helene's English seem fluent. Sinking into his bar stool, Callum gave up trying to follow the conversation Anne was having with Helene, instead focusing on the only other man in the place, the pianist, who besides being in the throes of a convivial tune, was not his type at all. Right. As if he was going to cock off in a lesbian bar. The idea made him smile, all the same.

Callum had never thought too hard about his attraction to men until he began noticing Anne's unending and ever-changing string of close female friends. He hadn't been the only one. A few years his senior, she'd in some ways taken the brunt of any scandal or judgement with headstrong dismissal, allowing him to find and explore beautiful boys without scrutiny, shielded by Anne's long shadow. He owed her, and if that meant sitting awkwardly, waiting for Anne to impress and probably collect her latest conquest for the rest of their night out, then that's what he'd do.

He slid his pfennigs over to the bartender as the beer appeared. She accepted them without a word, preferring instead to talk to another woman at the far end of the bar. Rather, the woman talked in her ear, between pointed glances at Callum. The bartender returned, leaning across the bar to mumble something to him in German.

"*Ein…einschubitte…*" He cursed himself for getting the word wrong immediately. "Sorry, I don't—"

"*Die Schatten, Die Schatten, bitte,*" she said, pointing not unkindly to a seat at the darker end of the bar.

Shadows? That much, he understood. He pleaded silently with Anne for intervention with a look she completely missed. Fine. He would wait, stuffed into a dark corner, finishing his beer in peace until she got tired of using that fake posh accent to impress the local *Mädchen* and was good and ready to leave.

It turned out *Die Schatten* weren't so bad for people-watching, and the beer was good and colder than it ever was back home. He hadn't yet learned to tell the German beers apart, or to match them up to the various names he'd seen about the bars in Kreuzberg. Engelhardt, Haase, Sacrau... Not that he'd make the mistake of asking for a specific one ever again. He'd asked for Bürgerliches at one place and the look of disgust the bartender had given him before a curt '*nein*' had been enough to dissuade him from trying to name any more of the local brews. Some young bloke with a wry smile and thickly veined arms had tried to bring it up to him after. He'd caught the name Bürgerliches, at least, but with no hope of understanding each other, Callum had settled for tucking a hand into the man's trousers, catching his mouth in a deep, hungry kiss, and enjoying their non-verbal, though far from silent night together. He'd had to borrow a few marks from Viktor to settle the bill in the morning. He should have known his luck with this Saxon beauty was too good to be true.

But at least tonight, his beer was cold.

He watched the piano player get up and collect his sheet music as a young woman dressed in a sharp tuxedo, her hair slicked back in the style that seemed popular here, replaced him. A couple of women cheered as the music sped up. A few even rose to dance on the small clearing in the floor. Callum wanted a cigarette. He reached for one, only to realise he'd left them in his coat, and no urge to smoke would persuade him to go another round with the surly bouncer.

"*Entschuldigung?*" he asked, getting it right this time as he made eye contact with the bartender. Unable to remember the word for cigarette, he mimed the action. She stared at him as if he were insane before holding up her hands to show she couldn't help. He was about to ask Anne for one when cold fingers stroked his chin. Startled, he turned to find their source, a young woman wearing a small black mask that looked more at home at a masquerade ball than in some Berlin dive. She extended a cigarette, gently placing it between his lips with a white-gloved hand. The glove was almost as white was her skin, or was that just the light? Perhaps the combination of the black mask, a tuxedo not unlike the pianist's and…! He'd never seen a woman wearing *black* lipstick. Callum knew Berlin to be a place of self-expression and recreation, but he'd never seen someone quite like this.

She dexterously snapped open a lighter and ignited his cigarette before disappearing into the crowd.

He was too dumbstruck to say thank you. He reached for another sip of his beer, trying to follow the woman through the crowd with his gaze. The place seemed to have swelled with women in the short time since their arrival. The music was louder too. And damn it, his beer was cold, and not just against the flesh of his palm and fingers. He could feel the chill rise through the back of his hand, up past his wrist, to—

He gasped, dropping the glass as the reflex overtook him. He leapt away from his seat as the glass hit the bar with a loud **thunk**, spilling beer as it rolled away. The bartender nimbly caught it and put it aside, its second **thunk** of the evening buried under a barrage of agitated German as she tried to mop up the mess that now dripped onto Callum's bar stool.

"Entschuldigung, entshuld…" he began, but trailed off as the damp cloth shrank to his skin. The bartender, Anne, and her date were all staring at him.

"Here," Anne said, snapping out of her disbelief long enough to hand the bartender a coin for her trouble, then waving Callum somewhere behind the dark corner to which he'd been banished.

Callum didn't wait for his audience to lose interest, disappearing into a small bathroom to survey the damage. He might have been wearing grey, but bloody hell! Anyone, even in a darkened club, could see the beer stain. It had even messed up his trousers.

He stripped off the damp shirt, folded it to where the stain began, wet it, and did his best to scrub it clean. Maybe he could get the smell out, and if he kept his jacket on at… No, the Eldorado was off the table now, not that he was in the mood.

He jumped as the door opened behind him, and a tall young man in brown trousers and a white string vest he definitely hadn't seen in the bar sidled up to the toilet beside him. Maybe he worked in the kitchen. Did the place have a kitchen?

"Hallo," the stranger said with a smile before unbuttoning his—

"He…hello." Callum looked away, suddenly aware he was staring.

As he emptied his bladder, the stranger took a good long look at Callum, who tried to smile when the man said something in German that sounded like a compliment. The man's gaze didn't move.

"*Danke*," Callum answered. He was still holding his shirt. "Oh! Umm… *Wasser? Und Bier*, actually."

"Ah." The stranger zipped up his trousers.

Callum stepped aside to let the man wash his hands. He frowned as the stranger then took the stained shirt and slipped it on himself.

"*Ist richtig?*" The man smiled, buttoning it up to the base of his chest, displaying himself proudly. Not only did it look good, it fit perfectly, which made no sense as the man had to have been a clear three inches taller than Callum. And the stain was nowhere to be seen.

Callum stared in amazement. "Yes, it… it's *richtig*."

"Ah, English." The stranger removed the shirt and tucked it into Callum's trousers. He then cupped a hand over Callum's groin, right where the beer had spilled. Callum opened his mouth to protest, only to have the German close his own mouth over it. He stroked Callum's chest, then the muscles of Callum's shoulders before letting go. "*Gut aus*… for English."

With a final wink, he was gone, leaving Callum to wonder what '*gut aus*' meant. The sooner he could afford a German teacher, the better. But his pants were dry. He stepped back and looked down at them, then up to the mirror, then at his pants again. He couldn't be that drunk on a few sips of beer.

The pants had been soiled, and now, they looked as good as new. He untucked the shirt from his trousers and opened it up. It was as clean and dry as it had been when he'd pulled it from his suitcase, only now it was less wrinkled. He put it around his back. It fit. He'd seen a man half a foot taller than him with a slimmer build put it on and it had fit the bastard perfectly. Now, it fit him again?

What the bloody hell were they putting in the drinks at this place?

He steadied himself against the sink, tucking the shirt in and checking his hair. He could still taste the man's cigarettes on his lips. Or were they his own? That woman… that woman in the mask had lit his cigarette, right before he dropped the glass.

To hell with it. He straightened his belt and returned to the club, trying to relax into the haze of smoke and the lively tunes of the piano, once more being played by a man. In fact, the place was full of men. The bar was the same, as were the dimly lit tables and chairs where now decidedly un-sapphic patrons huddled in twos and threes. The man who'd kissed him in the bathroom had a long arm wrapped around the shoulders of some other bloke as they talked with a third. More men dotted the dance floor in pairs, where at last, he saw a couple of… No, no, those weren't women. Had he come out the wrong door?

"Drink?"

Callum turned to the gruff voice to his left, where a burly man with a thick moustache had replaced the woman behind the bar. He nodded, not sure what he'd get in return for the pfennigs he fished from his pocket, or that it mattered.

His drink landed on the bar with a sharp thump. He pushed his coins toward the bartender, who stared at them with confusion, then left them there. Callum ignored yet another strange example of 'German service,' instead taking in the room once more. They were all around his age, if not younger. Most looked to be barely twenty. Strange. Such a pen of chickens usually lured the predatory stares and fat wallets of at least a few older gentlemen. More often than not, at least some of the boys were happy to oblige them.

"*Schön Abend?*"

He turned toward the smooth voice that had come from his right. The man it belonged to had a long scar that ran from the right side of his jaw up to his pronounced cheekbones. His blue eyes were bright and intelligent, and his light hair curled in a natural way that softened the angles of his face. Callum silently cursed himself for noticing the scar before anything else. Confused as he was, his *Abend* had certainly taken a turn of the *schön* kind.

"*Wie gehts?*"

"Uh, *ja*," Callum stammered. "*Ja, ja, wie gehts.* I mean, I'm well. Good. Yes... *Ja.*"

"Ah," the man answered, nodding with another smile. He stroked the back of Callum's hand with a soft finger and walked away. The international fairy's code for 'here ends our capacity for verbal dialogue.'

Callum wondered if it was possible to drown himself in a mug of beer. Where was Anne? Where were the lesbians? Whether this was his crowd or not, he'd embarrassed himself enough for one night.

The man weaved through the crowd, his light blue shirt easy to spot in a sea of white, cream, and grey. Callum's embarrassment soon found room for an encore, as the stranger sat down at the table with the friendly fellow from the bathroom. That was Callum's cue to leave… No, no, no, don't you—

His bathroom admirer waved his hand above the table, beckoning Callum over. The man in the blue shirt looked away shyly, but Callum could see him smiling. Great. All he wanted tonight was to be the sideshow at Chez Fritz. No thanks, lads.

He put his beer down on the bar and went to find the door or opening he'd come through that would take him back to Anne and the other women. No door. No curtain. Nothing of the kind in the bathroom either. This was asinine. He returned to his beer and lifted it to his lips. Maybe after a drink, he'd—

Callum pulled the sour brew away from his lips as if he'd burned them on it. Hell, he had! His lips and tongue felt numb. He tried to cry out, but only managed inarticulate grunts as his tongue failed to answer. A flash of blue crossed his vision, as the man who'd tried to talk to him earlier took hold of his chin, lifting it gently and blowing on Callum's mouth. Callum shivered so hard he felt like he'd burst, but there was no missing the brush of the stranger's cool lips on his, just for an instant, before his mouth cooled. He watched, regaining his breath as the man put a finger on the edge of his mug and circled its rim anti-clockwise. He then grazed the foam with his finger, before lifting it to Callum's lips, allowing him to suck the cool beer off it. It tasted normal. No nasty, boiling side effects. In fact, the mug seemed cooler in his hand.

The man whispered something to him in German, then returned to his table.

Callum took a sip just to make sure, tasting a cleaner, purer, colder pint than any pub had ever poured him. He couldn't help but stare at it, then at the scarred, blue-shirted stranger. The bar erupted in applause as the music stopped, and the small woman dressed in a tuxedo at the piano, the only woman in the place, stood up on the seat and bowed low. That mask… Callum recognised her immed—

"Where the hell were you?" Anne startled him, pulling on his shirtsleeve. "I waited, then spent an hour looking for you! Even popped in next door and let me tell you, I've now seen things no woman of virtue should. Someone should warn the nearest greengrocer. Also, we're running late now."

The room was again full of women. Not entirely the same women—Anne's date was gone—but the bar was back to its sapphic self.

"Hello? Are you going to answer me or not?"

"I… sorry, did you…?"

"Are you all right, darling? I thought you'd fallen in, and from the look of you, I wouldn't rule it out."

He thought about telling her. But what, exactly? Anne might have been the adventurous sort, but she was also practical. He couldn't imagine what she'd make of some half-cocked story about him visiting a full-cock bar in the short time he'd been away, never mind the rest of it. "I'm fine. Let's hurry. Where's…"

"Helene," Anne said after leaving him hanging for several seconds. "Such a bore. Hates the Eldorado, apparently. She might have told me that before! No matter. *We* are going to have the most fabulous time."

"F…f…fabulous?" he stammered.

"My dear cousin, you barely know the meaning of the word."

He let her guide him to the entrance to collect their coats, all the while looking back at the table in the corner, for any sign of a light blue shirt that was no longer there.

CHAPTER TWO

The sign above the door promising *Hier ist's Richtig!* confused Callum. It shone over the street like a layered puzzle, from the androgynous figure with the pencil moustache, to the 'come hither' eyes on the female opposite. The words *Hier ist's Richtig!* were duplicated in smaller, less cartoonish letters beneath, just in case visitors missed the garish main sign. Above it all, a spread fan hid the face of a young dancer behind a question mark that felt like a curiously German type of sarcasm.

"Here, it's right?" he asked Anne, trying to remember the basics Viktor had taught him as she pulled him toward the entrance.

"Oh, I don't know! What sort of question is that? You've arrived at the most marvellous place in the universe… Oh, do you have a couple of marks?

"What?"

"I loaned Helene money for a taxi."

"Loaned?" Callum fished the coins from his pocket, wondering if Anne would ever see Helene again. "Why did you bring us to a place that charges a mark just to get in?"

"Don't be a bore. You've simply no idea where you are—Oh!" She grabbed Callum's arm before he had a chance to object, giving a nod that was anything but discrete. "Don't stare, but do you know who that is?"

He looked over at the cluster of four well-cut suits she'd pointed out at a table across the way. "Should I?"

Anne rolled her eyes with drama. "That's Erika Mann and her brother, Klaus. You've heard of their father, Thomas?"

This time he did stare, blankly, at her.

"The novelist! *Death in Venice?* Surely, you've read it."

"No, and neither have you."

"Anyway, Erika was married to the actor, Gustaf Gründgens, though everyone knew it was Klaus he was sleeping with, including Erika, and she was too busy having it off with some other actress to mind. Now, they write and produce the most marvellous cabarets. Erika performs in them too! We must go and see one. Not sure who the two fellows are sitting with them. Writers too, I expect. It's that sort of place, besides the transvestites, who are their own sort.

"Transvestites?"

"Yes, isn't it darling? Do you think those fellows are English? They look English. Perhaps after a drink or two we should introduce ourselves? Oh, I love this place, don't you? It's just so..."

"*Richtig?*"

A tall woman pulled her cigarette holder out of their path with a smile. The shoulder of her dress fell from her shoulders. Not a woman, then. Callum didn't feign surprise. Even he'd not been so naïve as to miss the Eldorado's well-earned reputation as a 'daisy' safe haven.

"At last, she deigns to join our humble table."

Callum struggled to find the speaker in the dim light, until a freshly struck match lit the sharp jawline, delicate cheekbones and slick auburn hair of a young man. He ignited the cigarette of the dark-haired woman next to him, followed by his own.

Anne plonked herself down in a vacant chair next to the woman with the confidence of someone used to spending every night in the place. Callum gingerly took the seat next to her, spying a half-empty glass of white wine.

"He won't be long." The auburn-haired man gestured to another man in a stylish cream suit talking in earnest with a tall young fellow whose arm was draped around another. A marvellous place, indeed. "He's talking to Karl about something quite urgent, if I follow."

"It wouldn't hurt you to pay a little more attention," the dark-haired woman chided him.

"To politics?" The man ashed his cigarette with disdain. "Don't be ghastly. Introductions?"

"Of course! This is my cousin. Callum, this is Jacqueline and Robert." Anne accented the names with the kind of faux-Parisian precision only an English girl's school could cultivate.

"Hello." Callum extended a hand, which Jacqueline accepted with quiet amusement before Robert, the 't' in whose name was silent, took it with a perfunctory shake. "You're French?"

"*Enchanté*," Jacqueline answered with a smile.

"Jacqueline's from Spain, originally. Robert's from…" Anne trailed off, uncharacteristically unsure of her words. "I'm sorry, how common of me."

Robert finished for her. "Let's just say we travel."

"It's all right." Jacqueline squeezed Anne's hand, which seemed to fill her with relief. "Being an international woman of mystery can be so tiring, don't you think so, Anne?"

Callum smirked at the subtle barb, glancing at Robert's handsome features and getting only a bored expression in return. Suit yourself, tosser. "And he is…?"

The man in the tan suit appeared to be guiling the one called Karl about something. Callum watched them, sure that they were having the most important conversation in the room. More important than snatches of 'simply marvellous,' 'well I told you he was,' and 'a book about Berlin? How exciting,' at any rate.

"Callum?" Jacqueline asked. "Where exactly did you say you were from? Anne told us the North… I could well say the same, but in your case?"

"A terribly bourgeois question," Robert said through a smirk.

"I'm only curious. Please don't corner me into saying something condescending about 'the noble working class.'"

Robert flopped a pamphlet on the table. It was in German, of course, but Callum knew political propaganda when he saw it. "I've had quite my fill of working-class nobility for one night."

"Again? You'll exhaust that boy," Jacqueline said.

"Bold of you, to assume it's the same one. You wouldn't believe the number of young Marxists who are willing to give queer capitalism a try to pay for their beer and pussy."

"Do you have to use that word?" Anne asked. "It's so… euphemistic and ugly."

"Would you prefer cunt?"

"Oh, for pity's sake!"

"Are all the young blokes here…?" Callum searched for a word that wouldn't sound rude.

"On the game?" Robert rescued him. "You've no idea how bad it is in Germany, do you? I hope you haven't come looking for work."

"What does bring you to Berlin, darling?" Jacqueline took a long draw of her cigarette.

Again, Callum searched for an answer. His eyes fell on the manifesto, then darted to the man in the tan suit, then a coterie of broad-shouldered daisies in gartered stockings, then an overweight man in military dress who entered with two stern looking younger men flanking him.

"Dick," Anne answered for him, fairly spitting the word in Robert's direction.

Her candour shouldn't have shocked him by now. Still, Callum stared at her, until their table companions burst out laughing.

"Then you are in the right place," Robert raised his glass to Callum, his icy expression breaking at last.

Jacqueline, on the other hand, soured as the military men removed their coats and were escorted to a plush booth at the far side of the room. "Put that away," she said, sliding the manifesto back to Robert.

"What? It's just some Communist rubbish."

"Darling," she said again, nodding at the soldiers.

"What's the matter?" Anne grimaced as she spied the red armbands with the bent black symbol on them. "Why do they let them in?"

Robert tucked the pamphlet into his jacket, exchanging a look with Jacqueline. "Because that fat fuck always orders the most expensive champagne to pour down the throat of his latest boy toy in the hope it'll wash out the taste of Angry Chaplin's arse. Can we please not talk about politics? Callum, you're here for pleasure? Good job. There's plenty of that for all of us. Pay for it if you can, it's so much simpler. Don't worry if he's a hetter. Most have had enough practice to know what they're doing."

"Yes, well, you're the expert," Jacqueline smiled, waving to the man in the tan suit as he approached. "Frank? Is everything all right? Karl looked…"

The tall blond man introduced as Frank waved her enquiry away, resuming his seat behind the half-empty glass of wine and looking at Anne like she hadn't been two hours late. "Anne, nice to see you again."

"Frank? I want you to meet my cousin."

"Callum," he blurted, extending a hand with a blunt façade of confidence and hoping his fingernails were clean.

"Frank Bakker." The man smiled, taking him in a firm shake that belied his slight frame. "How are you enjoying Berlin?"

"It's all right." He hadn't just shrugged, had he? "I mean, it's great, yeah."

"Newcastle," whispered Jacqueline to Robert. "Perhaps Leeds."

"Definitely Leeds and you're doing it again," he purred back.

"Nottingham, actually," he corrected them.

Robert nodded. "I was closer."

"Still finding your feet, then?" Bakker continued, picking up his wine. "Are you here visiting Anne? How long are you staying?"

"Oh, questions, all these questions!" Anne scolded. "I'll order us a drink."

Callum shifted uncomfortably in his chair, hoping Anne would remember he preferred beer to any of the fancy poisons they probably served in this place. "I don't really know."

"An adventure, then?" Bakker asked, a non-guess meant to put him at ease. It somehow did the trick.

"I suppose you'd say that."

"And what have you seen so far? Brandenburg Gate? The Dom? A shame you didn't come in the summer. The Tiergarten is quite lovely then."

Callum had an odd sensation of the room falling away around him, as if Jacqueline, Robert, and everyone else in the club had faded into the background of some painting, while he held Frank's undivided attention. The touristic small talk should have bored him. But the curious glint in Frank's eyes made it oddly engaging. "It's a great city, yeah."

"And the bars?"

And there it was. Callum couldn't help but suspect their conversation had taken its first step on the road to mockery. "They're all right."

"All right, eh? *Richtig?*" Even as he said this, Frank's smile was kind. He tipped his wine toward Callum. "Just so long as you don't spend all your time in them. Or your money." The postscript had been tacked on in a way that reminded Callum how little he had, though again, not unkindly.

"I'm doing all right," he muttered.

"Well, good." Frank smiled. "You're in one of my favourite cities in the world. I'm glad to hear it's treating you well."

If Frank's demeanour had offered him some relaxation, the sense that eyes were following him from the far side of the room was its undoing. They peered at him from the middle of a squat, boar-like face, which was punctuated with one of those silly square moustaches, just below the man's bulbous nose. The man's two companions appeared not to notice, crying out raucously in German as shots of liquor disappeared down their throats.

"Pretend you haven't noticed them," Frank whispered to him.

"What?"

Jacqueline and Robert made a poor show of hiding the pause in their conversation, though a better one of hiding the fact that they too, now watched the Nazi's table with interest.

"Trust me, your night will go smoother," Frank continued.

Anne returned at that moment with two beers, setting one in front of Callum. "What's going on? Why are you all so quiet?"

Callum winced. She'd just been loud enough for the neighbouring tables to hear. When he shot another glance at the boar's table, the man had gone back to watching his two increasingly inebriated flunkies.

"That's Rohm, isn't it?" Callum asked. "I've seen him in the papers. Some politician or the like?"

"Some politician? He's head of the SA and all but bed chums with Angry Chaplin. Usually shows up with one or two of his more strapping meatheads, who stick close as long as he keeps the drinks flowing." Frank took another sip of wine. "You'll find far more interesting people in this room, Callum, I promise you."

"Hirschfeld for one," Jacqueline teased. Frank didn't bite.

"Oh, yes?" Anne piped up. "Doesn't he run that sex club? Or is it a university?"

Callum took a moment to parse the gap between these possibilities.

"Institute of Sexology," Frank answered. "Or the *Institut für Sexualwissenschaft* if you can get your mouth around it."

Anne snorted her drink.

Frank smirked. "That is not what I was implying. Anyway, Magnus may not be with us much longer."

Robert and Jacqueline looked at him with grim faces.

"Oh, nothing like that! Politics. Anyway, he may be enjoying the Institute's last throws. Von Papen's bad enough, but if… Anyway, Magnus seems very keen on moving his work to America."

"Why not?" Robert asked. "All the actors and directors have. Murnau, Dietrich… Veidt's hooked himself a Jew, so he'll no doubt be next."

"I thought we agreed, no politics?" Jacqueline reminded him.

"America," Frank continued. "Perhaps even Japan. I gather Magnus' ideas about sexuality have found some traction there."

"Must be so exciting, to travel so far!" Anne grinned, pulling the edges of her eyes back to lower their lids. "The mysterious east!"

"Don't do that," Callum chided her, gently pushing one of her hands away.

"What? You don't fancy me the next Anna May Wong?" She tilted her head from side to side in some mockery of a dance he supposed Wong had done in a film once.

"She's American, and you're embarr—"

"Chinese?"

"What?"

"I'm sure she's Chinese. Oh, wouldn't China be a marvellous adventure?"

"American, Chinese, Japanese, Siamese, Hawaiian... You're none of them."

Anne stuck her tongue out at him and sipped her beer. "It's far too easy to rile you up."

"A little too easy to rile everyone up these days." Frank shot another glance at Rohm's table, then returned his attention to Callum as if nothing was wrong. Callum refused to turn around. "You should come and see it for yourself."

"What? Japan?" Callum snorted.

"No," Frank laughed. "The Institute. Even if they're not forced to shut down, come Christmas, they'll no longer be doing tours."

"Always thought that was a ghastly business, anyhow," Robert growled. "Displaying our sex lives to Charlottenburg socialites? They can visit the bloody zoo."

"Magnus has always been about education first, you know that."

"Yes, don't be harsh, darling," Jacqueline chipped in. "It's not like Magnus is telling them precisely what that nice Communist boy has you put inside him."

Callum decided not to ask. He was sure he wouldn't be able to pronounce it, in any case. A loud bang and the sound of a breaking glass behind him made him turn around. He immediately wished he hadn't. Beyond the waiter with heavily rouged cheeks trying to clean up the spill, Rohm was staring at him again. Even as he sat with a thick arm around one of his handsome human Rottweilers, he never took his eyes off Callum.

"I'm so glad you've come!" Anne grabbed his arm with a delighted look in her eyes. "Berlin is just the place for both of us!"

Another commotion behind him made Callum risk another look. The younger Nazi shook off Rohm's arm with a scowl and disappeared behind a curtain Callum assumed led to the toilet. Rohm, for his part puffed at his cigarette, promptly transferring his affections to the other. His sights however, remained on Callum.

"He does like them a little rough," Frank explained with a conspiratorial smile.

"*Meine Damen und Herren!*" boomed a voice from the stage as the music lowered. More German followed that was well beyond Callum, as most eyes in the room settled upon the chubby man in the queer, short suit that now held court onstage. He told several jokes that set about half the crowd laughing, then went on some more, obviously talking up the star attraction.

"Oh, Cal, Cal, you'll love this!" squealed Anne, clapping her hands together with glee.

Callum watched the other Nazi slip from Rohm's clutches and follow his compatriot. Robert and Jacqueline watched as well.

"Let me guess," Jacqueline said. "The dark-haired one?"

"Huh?" Callum asked.

"A little game we play," Robert answered, watching the man disappear behind the curtain.

"Will you two pipe down?" Anne asked. "The show's about to start."

"Yes," purred Robert, getting up. "I think you're right."

Callum watched him follow the two men behind the curtain as a statuesque man in full glamour drag and an enormous blonde wig took the stage from the squat emcee.

"The best show is the people watching," Frank continued. "You'll be amazed how much you learn."

"I can see that," he answered, sheepishly.

The man gave him another kind smile. "Look, Callum, I know this is all very new to you, but how would you feel about coming to the Institute for one of their tours on Saturday afternoon?"

"T…tours?"

"It might be the last chance you get. And I think you'll be quite amazed by what Magnus is doing for… well, people like us."

Like us? Robert had been far from subtle, and anything went with the Frenchies, but Frank, also? And how did Frank know he liked lads? He was about to deny it, but there seemed little point. In any case, lying to the man felt wrong. Something about him, whether it was an intelligence Callum wasn't used to rubbing shoulders with, or just his kindness, he *wanted* to tell Frank more. He waited for Anne to stop vigorously applauding and tilted his empty beer glass. "Yeah, all right. I'll think about that."

"Please do. I think you'll find it most enlightening." Frank smiled, turning his attention to the show.

Callum watched the performer strut the stage, all too masculine muscles bulging out of her sparkling gown as she warbled in German. A moment later, some tiny bloke in an enormous top hat and oversized tails waddled out on stage and took her in a ridiculous slow dance. Anne roared with laughter, while Jacqueline and Frank chuckled. Robert was nowhere to be seen.

"I'll get us some more drinks." Callum gestured to Frank's empty glass.

"With what?" the man quipped before dropping three marks on the table.

Feeling foolish and trying to smile gratefully, Callum took them, moving to the bar as the singer spun her unlikely partner around and around, faster and faster until his heels clipped the curtains, and her singing grew increasingly breathless. At last, she set him down on the stage, where he staggered around under his ridiculous hat before falling on his backside like he was Buster Keaton. The crowd roared again. Callum just didn't get it. Or maybe Rohm's stare was pissing him off. Should he say something? No, everything he'd ever heard about the SA told him that was a terrible idea. And now, he needed to piss. The drinks could wait.

He pushed back the curtain where Robert had disappeared moments before, and walked straight into a dark-haired youth whose chest muscles heaved under his brown shirt, simmering on the edge of rage. The man barked a furious slew of German and shoved Callum against the wall.

"Aye! Sorry mate, I didn't see you." Callum got out, trying not to stare at the red armband which looked back through him, a quartet of broken black limbs at its centre.

The man gave him one last shove and stormed off. Then the other, taller and blond, looked Callum over with a smirk. Or was he leering at him? Callum didn't look the brute in the eye. He could fight his way through any common thug well enough, but two? He wasn't about to push his luck.

"English?" the blond asked, as if the word were a damning curse.

Callum nodded.

"More careful next time, eh?" The man playfully slapped his jaw, then stalked out after his colleague.

Now, Callum really needed to piss. He pushed another curtain aside to find Robert nursing a bloody nose over the sink.

"What the hell happened to you?" he asked.

The smooth-tongued traveller rolled his eyes, wincing as if it pained him. "You should see the other one."

"I think I just did. Here." Callum reached for one of Robert's hands.

"Don't… touch it. It looks worse than it is."

"Why? What did you say to them?"

"What does anybody say to them?" Robert asked, at last giving Callum a view of the vicious cut below his eye where the thug had jabbed him. "I suggested some amusement. It seems Rohm has outbid me. Unfortunately, the only thing emptier than those boys' souls is their wallets."

"You tried to chat up a Nazi? Are you daft?"

"Good fellow, I've no illusions about the risks that come with seeking satisfaction in the body of a bigot, but don't knock it 'til you've tried it. You'd be surprised how many of them will oblige."

Callum was not yet ready to put a bloody nose and a night of bigoted passion on his list of Berlin must-dos. "Are you sure you're—?"

"Oh, stop fussing! And please don't tell me you came back here just to check on me. But… thank you."

Unzipping as he approached the trough, Callum remembered a joke he'd heard when he'd first arrived. 'German beer in, English beer out.' He'd laughed at the time. "How long have you been in Berlin?"

"What's that?"

"How long have—"

"Oh…" Robert paused. "Two years? Three? It's the sort of place one tends to lose track, even of one's own business.

Makes a change from Paris, where every acquaintance makes it their business to keep track of yours."

Callum zipped up, returning to the sink to wash his hands. "You should still get that looked at. At least tell someone."

"Rohm would have this place shuttered within hours if anybody raised a scene. Unfortunately, that does give his bully boys a certain ego. They weren't like that in the old days. Angry, yes, but it was all about the economy. Then came the rhetoric, then someone to blame."

"You sound more worried than you sa…" Callum trailed off, glimpsing Robert's face in the mirror. No. He couldn't be! "You're all right?"

Robert rolled his eyes. "For the last time—"

"No, I mean your eye." He couldn't see the cut anywhere, nor any bruising.

Robert wiped the last of the blood from his face and washed it away at the sink. "It's as I told you, not as bad as it looks."

Robert left the room without another word. The dim sound of the show outside pierced the curtains, but otherwise, Callum was left to stare at his reflection. He looked pale, like his skin had thinned somehow. So, this was the Eldorado? Free-flowing booze, transvestites, daisy boys and thugs given a free hand? Maybe there was a door or curtain here that would lead him to another cosy pub, ideally one full of working lads he could actually talk to, though he would have taken a solitary beer at a pinch. What did it matter if he only imagined it? And he *had* imagined it.

Why was he even here? Because the wrong 'working lad' back in Nottingham would likely belt him around the mouth for a misplaced look. It had happened, once even after Callum had taken a mouthful from the nasty prick. But there were places to find working lads in Berlin who wouldn't turn him down with their fists. As long as he steered clear of its loony radicals and bully-boy peacocks, this was the place. Berlin, not the Eldorado. *Hier ist's richtig?* Not for him.

He made good on his promise to pick up drinks and returned to the table where Anne, Robert, Jacqueline, and Frank watched the clown show unfolding on stage with rapt attention. That's all the crossdressers on stage were, really. Clowns in skirts. Callum didn't see why people at home got their knickers twisted over a bit of silly fun that did no more harm than a Christmas panto. The woman in the oversized hat and man's suit peeled off her moustache and stuck it on the tall singer's face. It slid off immediately with a dusting of heavy pancake makeup. The queen looked shocked. The crowd roared with approval. The suited woman bowed, then, holding a bottle of champagne between her legs, took aim at the queen's mouth, and fired.

The audience, Callum's table included, lost their minds, *Hier ist's richtig!* fulfilling its promise at last. The only table not getting into the fun was Rohm's. The man's piggish eyes fixed on the scowl that darkened the face of the dark-haired soldier… the one who'd hit Robert, Callum guessed. The blond, for his part, seemed bored with it all as his eyes followed a waitress carrying a tray of schnapps shots. Or was it a waiter? The blond leered in a way that suggested he didn't care either way. At last, the darker one got up and with a small, reluctant nod to his superior, made to leave. The blond tried to dissuade him, but Rohm waved them both away, focusing once more on the show. Callum felt something in his gut unclench as the two went to leave, but just as they reached the door, both turned. Whatever had relaxed a second ago within Callum now sank as both men stared at his table. Then, with as little warning, they turned and left the club without a word.

As the emcee took the stage again, Callum kept his eyes on the door as if expecting the men to return, perhaps with company. But they didn't. When he turned around, Robert and Jacqueline were standing to leave.

"You're not staying for the next act?" Anne asked them. "Oh pooh, that's no fun."

"Urgent business elsewhere, *ma chérie*." Jacqueline kissed her on the cheek.

"Callum," Robert said coolly, shaking his hand before giving Anne a farewell kiss as well.

"Hope to see you again soon," Jacqueline said, kissing him just short of his cheek in that weird way Europeans did. No kisses were exchanged with Frank.

"Did you say something to upset them?" Anne asked, watching the pair leave.

Frank shook his head. "Those two keep their own hours. So, Callum, how about that tour? I believe there's one at the Institute on Saturday."

Callum took a long draw of his beer as a pair of surely-not-women took to the stage playing clarinets. "I… I don't know. I don't know much about that sort of thing."

Frank leaned forward and put a gentle hand on his. "My friend, that's the whole point."

"All right then. I suppose."

"Splendid." Frank jotted down the address on a white card and slid it to him. "Three o'clock, and don't be late. This is still Germany. They're a permissive lot, but punctual."

Callum took the address, after which the man had scrawled *Tiergarten* in parenthesis, and tucked it into his pocket. He could feel Rohm's eyes on him again. "If you don't mind, I think I'll... Anne?"

"Oh cousin, really? We've only just arrived."

He shook his head, feeling all but invisible as she bopped along to the jaunty tune.

Frank offered him a sympathetic smile. "I'll see that Anne pours herself safely into a taxi, don't worry. I know the nightlife can take some getting used to. But we'll see you again?"

"Yes, Saturday?" Callum hoped he didn't seem too eager, but he had been invited.

"Saturday it is," Frank answered with a satisfied nod. He shook Callum's hand warmly as they stood up, then leaned across the table and kissed his cheeks three times.

Callum straightened his spine, a little startled.

"Until then," Frank said warmly, resuming his seat and turning back to the show.

CHAPTER THREE

Callum gathered his coat at the entrance and stepped out onto the street, unable to remember where they'd left the U-Bahn. Berlin was as bad as London for disorienting streets, and now it was snowing, nothing looked the same. Had they crossed the main street? Which one was that? He picked the quietest option and started walking. He needed to be away from people for a while, and if he walked an hour or more in the wrong direction, who cared? Anne would be fine. He'd be out from under Rohm's gaze. He ignored the laughter that spilled from one of the nearby pubs as a man disappeared inside it. All illegal, but all thriving. Unlike the busy-bodies back home, he guessed the Germans had bigger problems than trying to police fairy boys.

He spied a group of three more Brownshirts a few doors up, coming his way. With no particular destination, he turned up a side street, then into a quieter laneway after that, only to hear the muffled groans of two men enjoying one another in the darkness. The sound of faint whimpering in German suggested a good time in full swing, at least, until one stared right at him, bright eyes filled with lust. But it was more than that. The man's expression bordered on a loss of control, like whatever he was doing with his alley companion had awakened in him some uncontrollable animal instinct to mate… or feed.

Callum stumbled backward, almost falling in the snow as he recognised Robert. He saw the stain across Robert's mouth, the long, sharp teeth that withdrew from the neck of the dark-haired SA thug, whose head lolled toward him in a half-drunken stupor. The steady drip, drip into the snow left no doubt, the man was bleeding from the neck.

Callum turned and ran, only to see Jacqueline a little way up the lane, the slumped body of an SA man at her feet. She tilted her head, at last giving him a full view of her face, also stained with blood.

"Darling," she murmured. "Leaving us so soon?"

He bolted for the street from which he'd come. The trio of SA shouted something at him as he rushed past, but there was no catching up to him. Callum could run, snow or no snow. Perhaps the three men would share the fate of their comrades. But what was that, exactly? What had he just seen? Was it a trick, or some silly Berlin sex game they'd played on him?

Silly Berlin sex game? Was he going mad? He knew blood when he saw it!

"Callum!"

He spun to face the voice, but there was no-one there. Yet, he'd as good as felt it, inches from his ear, almost inside his head! They'd find him. There was no such thing as 'fast enough.' Somehow, he knew they'd find him.

He looked around for somewhere safe. Damn it, safe from *what?*

The bright lights of a passing car reflected off the snow, revealing a series of doors he recognised. The women's bar! They wouldn't look for him… Hell, they weren't *looking* for him! They could speak directly to his mind. They'd find him, all right.

Unless…

He ignored odd looks from the last few women gathered around the tables in the bar's darkest corners. He also ignored the bartender's scowl as she grunted something at him in German.

"*Entschuldegung, Fraulein…*" he began, not sure how to continue.

"Closing," she said, firmly, pointing to the clock behind the bar. It was close to midnight.

"Please?" he asked, somewhat piteously. "*Ein Bier? Bitte?*"

She shrugged, fetching him a glass. At this time of night, a pint sold was a pint sold. The woman mumbled the total and Callum dumped a few pfennigs from the change he'd collected at Eldorado. He'd meant to give it back to Frank. That Rohm bastard had distracted him. Then, he'd seen bigger monsters make short work of Rohm's bully boys. Monsters, who moments before had kissed him goodnight and told him to enjoy Berlin like a happy little tourist. He stared into the bubbles of his beer, waiting for what? For more of the voice that had invaded his head? The one he couldn't quite attribute to either Jacqueline or Robert, but which had rattled his nerves all the same? Were they coming? Would they find him here? Would something *worse* find him here? The bartender gave him another odd look.

Right. Closing. Bollocks.

He took a long pull of his drink. He needed more than a beer, but didn't want to push his luck trying to order something stronger, and he had never developed the taste, nor the stomach for schnapps. He had… three minutes? He jumped as the door banged behind two women leaving the bar. All right, think, you jittery bastard, think!

He snatched up his beer and disappeared once more into the toilets, where he could at least be left alone. If they came looking for him in this place, already a big 'if,' they wouldn't—

They're already in your head, idiot!

He caught a glimpse of himself in the mirror again, looking even less healthy than before. He looked like he ought to be in bed. Maybe more to drink wasn't a great idea. He barely noticed the glass slip from his fingers until it hit the floor with a loud crack and shattered. Beer-soaked shoes to match his beer-soaked shirt. Welcome to fucking Berlin.

Had someone turned up the music outside? He frowned, certain now that he could hear a vibrant piano being played, instead of the somewhat sombre record the bartender had put on to kick out her last regulars. Unless… No, he'd imagined all that, hadn't he?

Just as he was imagining it now.

Dandy boys stepping together in intimate embrace on the dance floor, another in shabby looking coat tails providing musical accompaniment, and the same gruff, barrel-shaped bartender who'd refused his coin. The place seemed even busier, though not so busy he couldn't recognise the scarred young man in the blue shirt. The one who'd somehow cooled his drink, then kissed him.

He had to leave. Then never come back to this place where they put God knew what in the drinks! That had to be it. He'd imagined this bar, he'd imagined the voice in his head, and he'd imagined the two faces stained with Nazi blood. It was late. He'd gotten lost. The lights, liquor, and cold had disoriented him, and it was time to go home. He'd walk all the way back to Neukölln if he had to.

He crossed the room and pushed back the curtain that concealed the front entrance, only to be greeted with the same wood panelling that covered the sides of the room. No handle. No doorknob. Not even a window.

The scarred man smiled at him. Callum didn't know why he smiled back. The stranger was not such a bad illusion, but he was an illusion, just the same.

He'd come in through the toilets, hadn't he? Easing his way through the crowd, he returned, finding the room empty, to his relief. In the mirror, he stared at his own reflection, face full and healthy as it had ever been, freshly shaven at Anne's insistence, which made Callum look more boyish than probably suited him. But he'd looked nothing like this in the real bar. It so shocked him, he barely noticed the piano, still playing, not getting any softer as he stared.

"Eine schöne Aussicht?"

Callum turned to the voice that had come from his right. "Eh?"

The scarred man smiled with only half his face, which Callum soon realised was all he could manage, probably due to the same injury that had caused the scarring. The stranger rocked lightly on the balls of his feet, like a shy boy unsure what to say to a girl he fancied. Or to a boy he fancied.

The man drew closer, pausing as he stood inches from Callum's face. He sniffed the air. *"Bier?"*

Why not? *"Bitte,"* Callum said, before remembering the beer that had soaked through his shoes into his sock. Did the stranger mean to offer or was he commenting on the smell? Callum could smell it, which made the whole illusion seem more real. Perhaps he'd hit his head.

The fellow grinned, tilting his head to the curtained entrance.

Where else did he have to be? Callum followed the man past the young guys sitting at the bar. Several were already dancing, arms around one another in a way Callum had never seen before coming to Berlin. They were all so young. Excluding the bartender and the pianist, barely a handful looked over twenty-five, and those that did would have been thirty at a stretch. Yet there were few unblemished beauties. Callum saw at least two eye patches, one man limping towards the bar, hands that were missing fingers, and countless scars, some much more serious than those on his suitor.

Suitor? Well, listen to you, all posh and hoity, he thought.

Something in him seized up as he approached his new friend's table, where the same group of friends now looked up and stared at him with a faint mix of curiosity and amusement. The new novelty at Chez Fritz.

"You found him again?" asked a friendly-looking dark-haired fellow whose slender frame was drowning in an off-white shirt. Sitting next to the bloke in the string vest, the one who'd tried on Callum's shirt and kissed him in the toilets, the speaker looked like a pirate captain drinking with his mate.

"*Hallo,*" Callum said, trying to keep the quiver out of his voice. "*Wie gehts?*"

The man grinned as all eyes at the table landed on their guest. "You speak a little German, then?"

Callum smiled shyly. "Only what I've learned since I came here."

"Ah, but do you know where 'here' is?"

He didn't know how to answer that. The gregarious German spared him further embarrassment with a flurry of introductions. There was Oskar, and Ernst, then Johann, the flirty, vest-wearing rogue… and finally the scarred blond man in the blue shirt, Max.

"Callum," he got out, nodding at each of them and catching a dark look from Ernst.

"Sit with us, Callum?" the English-speaker who'd introduced himself as Ferdi asked. "There is room next to Max, I think?"

Johann smirked, moving to make said room while Max shot Ferdi an embarrassed glare. Well, it wasn't as if Callum could refuse now. He took the vacated space, at last noticing Ferdi's mismatched eyes, one a deep, natural brown, the other a surreal green, like glass. A small piece of his ear was missing too, like a cat who'd been through a street fight. A pirate cat? Callum wanted to laugh, but instead looked away quickly, only to notice burn scars under Ernst's collar, and a long gash along Oskar's head which divided his crop of thick red hair. Only

Johann appeared to be without some injury. Not one of them could have been more than twenty-five.

Max recovered quickly from his embarrassment, smiling at Callum and rubbing the back of his hand before taking another sip of his beer. Without words, the gesture undid the knot that had formed in Callum's stomach, even if they were all still staring at him. And they *were* still staring.

"How long have you been in Berlin, Callum?" Ferdi asked. "And from where?

It was an obvious question, but he had to start somewhere. "A month. I'm from Nottingham."

Ferdi translated for his friends.

"Robin Hood?" Johann laughed, then mimed firing a bow and arrow.

"That's the one." Callum forced a smile like he hadn't heard the joke a hundred times since arriving. He hadn't expected Germans to be so obsessed with folk stories of English outlaws. More likely, it was all they'd heard about Nottingham.

Ernst said something curt to Johann that cut short his laughter. Johann fired something back, giving him a dismissive wave. Ferdi's attempt to intercede seemed the last straw, as Ernst slapped his fingers down on the table with a bang and stalked off to the bar.

"*Drama-Kind,*" Oskar muttered, sipping his beer.

Johann glared at him, then turned to Callum, shaking his head apologetically. "Ernst... hate English. Sorry."

"He what?" Callum didn't know why this caught him so off-guard. He'd been only seven when they'd signed the armistice. When Germany's slide into economic oblivion had begun. "I'm sorry."

"*Nein,*" Ferdi waved his apology away. "We were all the same then, obeying cruel, selfish little men, trying to protect their empires. We are all the same now."

Max muttered in German something which set Oskar and Johann laughing.

"The Communists are as stupid as the rest," Ferdi retorted. "But they have it right when they say 'no gods, no masters.' Anyone who calls himself master will soon face a revolution of his own stupid making."

Johann pursed his lips and blurted out a march while miming a trumpet. "*Revolution!*"

More laughter. Max squeezed Callum's hand again, then relaxed, his touch sending a jolt up Callum's wrist to the pit of his gut. No… lower.

Ferdi looked over at the sulking Ernst, then said something in German to Johann, who gave them a rueful smile and went over to his friend by the bar. When he tried to put his arm around Ernst, the man shook it off.

"Drama," Oskar whispered again with a mischievous smile.

Callum wasn't sure if Max's body had drawn closer to his, or if it was just his own temperature rising. The man's breath smelled so sweet on Callum's face that he was scared to make eye contact.

"*Entschuldegung*," Oskar said at last, leaving them for a lad he'd spied on the other side of the room. And then there were three.

Ferdi smirked at Max. "*Er ist schön.*"

Callum knew he'd just been paid a compliment, even as they exchanged a few more words that weren't translated for him. It was probably best not to know. He was nervous enough. He kept forcing himself to look away from Ferdi's green eye.

"You like it?" the man asked, his attention now firmly drawn.

"*Nein*," Max said sharply, as if to head off a scene, or some kind of grisly party trick. "Ferdi, *nein!*"

Ferdi grinned, moving a hand closer to his eye as if to... Ew!

Callum felt Max's hands close quickly around the sides of his face, hiding whatever Ferdi was about to do. The entire bar, with all its bright music, revelry and dancing disappeared beyond the fleshy cave that hid them from the world. Callum was sure he heard Ferdi laugh, and possibly say something, but it was hard to care. Max's skin was too soft, his breath far too sweet for a man who'd spent hours drinking. In fact, Callum couldn't smell the two or three beers he'd seen Max down at all. He smelled more like a queer mix of fresh cream and honey. When Max's lips brushed his, he could no longer resist. They tasted as good as they smelled.

And the taste was entirely new. It was not as if Callum had never felt the touch of a man's lips or tongue on his before. But it had never felt easy, nor right like this. The shame he'd felt in those moments seemed as far now from his mind as

Berlin, or the chance to kiss a man this way in public had when he'd nursed beers at The Dancing Fox in Nottingham, stealing looks at the blokes still in factory kit, all caked in grime. Twice, such a man had caught him looking and not pretended otherwise. Both of those men had tasted of sweat, grease, pain, piss, and rage. They'd never kissed him, and he'd never have dared ask, not even once they'd spent themselves in his mouth. Get knob. Get off. Get out of my sight, yer fairy. No want, just convenience. The second one had thumped him just to make sure they were clear.

With the working boys he'd met during his short stay in Berlin, there had been want, for his body, and sometimes money he couldn't spare. With Max, the want was pure and real. The want for Callum. He wasn't sure how he recognised the difference, but it shone clear as bright hot summer to him now. That jolt that went far deeper than his skin, or even his prick.

"*Schön?*" he whispered.

"*Sier schön,*" his admirer answered, kissing him again, "for English."

That made Callum laugh, though he didn't know why. It normally pissed him off when the locals mocked him for not understanding either their language or customs. Even Anne annoyed him sometimes, pretending she knew it all. But nothing about Max's tease had been unkind. The gentle squeeze of the man's hands around Callum's confirmed it.

Max suddenly appeared to notice his lack of a drink, turning to him with shame. "*Bier? Kindl? Weiss?*"

"Um…" Callum pointed to Max's near empty glass. "Same?"

Ferdi waved a polite refusal.

Max grinned, getting up to go to the bar. Callum noticed there were no waiters in the place. Not even a boy collecting empty glasses. Yet, there were also no empty glasses. Well, he had to be imagining this now, hadn't he? But the touch of Max's skin? His sweet breath? Callum knew his imagination wasn't that vivid.

"He's sweet, yes?"

Callum hadn't noticed Ferdi sidle up next to him. Hell, from the moment he'd been invited to sit at their table, he hadn't seemed to notice much. "Uh, I suppose he is."

"What's wrong? You don't like boys?"

"I like… men."

"But they're still new to you? You are afraid?"

"I'm not afraid. I…" Why not admit it? He was relatively new to this. "Berlin's quite the place."

Ferdi agreed with a warm nod. "It would be nice to see it again."

The strange reply convinced Callum he'd misunderstood. "Where are you from?"

Ferdi grinned. "Here."

"You're a Berliner?"

The man shook his head. "Here is where I'm welcome. I was born in Bremen if that is what you mean. You know Bremen?"

"Like the animal musicians?"

"Yes," Ferdi laughed. "Everyone knows the animals, like we know your Robin Hood."

Callum flinched as Ferdi put a hand on his, though the man took care not to touch him with the same affection Max had. He also frowned.

"What is it?" Callum asked.

"You're fortunate. Your scars are hidden, like Johann."

"My what?"

Ferdi turned his head, allowing the light to shine off his glassy green eye and catch his ruined earlobe. "I'm not ungrateful. I'm fortunate too."

Callum flicked his gaze around the bar, feeling uncomfortable under Ferdi's sudden scrutiny. Again, few of the men inside seemed untarnished by injury. One face turned toward him whose skin looked worn through, raw as muscle. He caught himself in a breath.

Ferdi squeezed his hand, leaning close to whisper. "It's polite to show your scars here, at least once."

Before Callum could ask, Ferdi was across the bar, chatting up some youngster in a white vest with a lopsided smile. It was a look closer to the one Callum was used to seeing in Berlin.

Max placed a beer in front of him as he sat down. As Callum reached for it, Max gently stopped him, reached for the glass himself, and touched its rim. Callum watched the foam agitate a little before Max withdrew.

"*Ist besser?*" the man asked.

Right. Because his first sip of a drink in this place had near set his throat on fire. *"Danke."*

Max grinned at him again, squeezing his thigh. They watched the crowd, soft touch their only communication. But the silence allowed Callum's mind to wander, back to what he'd seen in the alley. Brownshirt thugs. Blood on the snow. Why this bar had no door. How sick he'd looked in the mirror. The beautiful scarred boy next to him… Always, his thoughts would come back to the man next to him. How? After what he'd just seen and the night he'd had? The promised wonders of the Eldorado barely earned a cameo in his memory.

"Is all right?" Max asked, stroking Callum's chin.

"Yes, I…" What was he supposed to ask? Where did he get the scars? Why was a women's place now filled entirely with men? Why did those men all seem to have scars? Why the drinks? Why, why, why… It seemed the most useless word in the English language to him now, and he wasn't convinced its German equivalent would be much more help.

Did Max believe in monsters?

The crowd cheered as the music switched to a jaunty, big-band number.

"Danse?" Max asked, grabbing his hand.

If 'why' was a useless word to him, 'dance,' in any language, had to be one of the most terrifying. But as he shuffled around the tiny floor near the now silent piano, where a dozen or so men including Ferdi and his companion each made their own awkward attempt at keeping rhythm, he overcame his nerves, as if some glorious dream had swept over the bizarre events of the past hour or two. Unless those events had been the dream. Frankly, he would have preferred Max, Ferdi, and this place where men danced without care as to what the world thought of them to be real. But who was to say otherwise? He could feel it and taste it. It had a distinct smell and a heat that wrapped around him, not like he belonged, exactly, but like he belonged for now, enough to be seen and felt in a way he hadn't been since…

Max drew closer as the music slowed. He saw others drift away from the dance floor, retreating to their tables, friends, drinks and lovers… 'You like Max?' Ferdi had asked him. In as much as he could like a man he'd just met, yes, he liked Max a lot.

That didn't put him at ease with the way Ferdi was looking at him. The look was more measured, more thoughtful and curious than the scorn that had sent Ernst from their table in a huff. Ferdi seemed to be studying Callum. Callum had never much liked study in school, and he liked it as a subject even less. It gave him another reason to focus on Max. Max wasn't studying him. Max just leaned his head against Callum's, his sweet breath breaking over Callum's lips until they finally kissed, deep, open, and unbothered in the way Callum had seen his school chums kiss their girls when they thought no-one was looking. He'd barely been able to think about kissing another man like that, and when he had… To hell with thought. This was pure feeling, and it made him want to pull Max closer.

The man's grin dimpled the scars on his young face, giving him an innocent, roguish charm as his blue eyes stared into Callum's, golden hair catching the dim light. "I think I'm dreaming."

It was a foolish, school boy sentiment, but it made Callum pull even closer, as if he was being hugged from the inside. Was this what it was to have a man want you for more than just getting off? This, from a man he barely knew. Hell, *didn't* know. Perhaps they were both dreaming. Dancing together in their dreams. That's why this felt the way it did. The lights seemed to dim, and Callum realised Max had guided him away from the dance floor to a darker corner of the room to kiss him again, alone and in private. And kiss him, Max did, with longing, as if he were searching for Callum's deepest secrets, or could even dissolve his shame. But Callum didn't feel shame now, just the curves of Max's slim body, as the man opened the top two buttons of his shirt. Were they allowed…? Oh, screw 'allowed!' He felt Max's cool, sweet breath whisp through the hairs of his chest, before the man's hand slipped into his shirt. He leaned closer for another kiss.

Max paused, frowning for the first time. Was Callum being too eager? Had he caused offense? Been too easy a conquest? Max's cool hands pawed under his shirt, stroking his flank, his stomach, his chest, as if searching for something. Then, far more abruptly than he'd entered, Max withdrew, staring at Callum with what now, even in darkness, could only be confusion and horror.

"*Fleisch?*" he asked, the word barely more than a breath. "*Bist Fleisch?*"

Callum shook his head. "I don't know what you mean."

"*Fleisch!*" Max's eyes were wide as Ferdi rushed over to them. "*Ist Fleisch!*"

Ferdi shushed Max, putting an arm around his shoulders. He shot a rueful look at Callum, who felt all the safety, warmth, and welcome the place had offered evaporate as Ferdi and Max's eyes bore into him. *Fleisch?* The word stung like a curse. He shook his head again, but the two men didn't move. Max stared at him, slack-jawed until at last Ferdi spoke.

"Callum, you have to go!"

He didn't need to be told twice. But go where? The toilets? It had been his only way in and out of here so far. Ignoring the stares, he retreated without another word, throwing himself through the curtain to find the small room mercifully empty. He let the curtain fall behind him, neared the sink, and waited, staring at his pink, heaving reflection, a great hunkering pile of… *Fleisch?* Did that mean what it sounded like? He waited. Waited for the music to die down. It only grew louder and louder, until it flooded his ears and he craved the quiet of the closing girl bar. He needed it. Any kind of quiet. His puffy pink face taunted him from the mirror, on the verge of tears. But for what? A dream? This whole bloody night had been a dream! Monsters in the street? Max? The bar? He wanted to wake up, damn it, if he had to bash his head against the damn mirror to do it.

Whether the thought had manifested, or he'd simply gone mad, the pain lasted only a second before Callum lost consciousness, barely tasting his own blood.

CHAPTER FOUR

"Good morning."

Callum shielded his eyes from the sudden glare as Anne pulled back the curtain. He winced at what felt like the grinding lethargy of a brutal hangover. Anne's voice, gentle and cheery as she was, wasn't helping.

"If you can stay awake this time, I'm making some tea." She squeezed his wrist. "You gave us an awful fright."

What? Where? Why? None of these questions got past 'Wh…' on Callum's lips.

"You don't remember?" Anne asked. "I don't know what inspired you to go back to Suzi's after, but it's a good job you did. She's such a doll."

"Suzi?" The face of the decidedly un-doll-like bartender came back to him.

"I suppose I must have told her we were off to the Eldorado. Anyway, she ran all the way there when she found you. Barely caught us! Good job Frank knows his way around bandages and a pair of scissors."

That explained the pressure around his head. His fingers brushed the rough cloth.

"No concussion, or at least Frank doesn't think so. I told him we should take you to a hospital, but he was dead against the idea. Something about the economy, hospitals not being as good as they used to be and worse if you're not German. I suppose he knows what he's talking about. They do have the most marvellous word for hospital here, though. *Krankenhaus.* Isn't that good? It's so much fun to say."

"Hospital?" He wondered if she'd even heard. "What the hell?"

"Your head? Suzi found you on the floor. A bit of a bloody mess, I'm afraid, but it's all right now. Frank's coming by in a bit to check on you."

"I'm at your place?"

Anne retreated as whistling came from the tiny kitchenette. "Of course! I obviously can't let you out of my sight for a minute."

The smell of warm tea washed over the shabby damp of Anne's room as Callum laboured to sit up.

"Slowly, slowly," she said, patiently handing him the tea when he was settled.

"Where did you sleep?"

She tilted her head toward an armchair that had seen better days. "Don't mind me. I can nod off anywhere."

He sipped gratefully and smiled. "Tell Suzi 'thank you.' I'll pay for the mirror."

Anne frowned. "What mirror?"

The one he'd hit his head on? He wasn't sure now.

"Damn it, I told Frank, a hospital! If this business has sent you loopy, I won't forgive myself, or him."

"I'm… I'm fine. Really, I am. Dreaming, I suppose."

"Fine," she said, sipping her tea. "Maybe you should tell me what you do remember."

As the familiar, bittersweet flavour washed over his tongue, Callum began to remember a lot. The alley, the Nazis, the bathroom, the bar, Max… especially Max. Except, none of that had been real. It couldn't have been real.

"*Fleisch*."

"What's that?"

He'd spoken without realising it. "Just something I remembered."

"From the dream? *Fleisch* is just meat. Or flesh, I suppose. What's that mean?" she asked, her voice finally betraying her Midlands roots.

"I… don't worry. I don't know why I said it."

"Well, there's no *Fleisch* here, but you should probably eat something. Use that same charming effect you had on Frank when he arrives."

"Charming?"

Her gaze whipped disappointment across him. "Oh, darling."

The loud buzz erupted from near Anne's door. Still in her nightgown, she threw a coat over her shoulders and disappeared through. When she returned, Frank was a step behind, dressed in a well-cut grey suit, dark overcoat slung over one arm, clutching a small paper bag. He looked a sight in Anne's modest digs, particularly when she tossed off her housecoat and lit a cigarette. She eased open a window and sat by it, watching as Frank set the bag in the kitchen and approached Callum.

"How are you feeling?" the man asked.

"He's been a sparkling conversationalist," Anne tossed in, her 'society' affect back in place. "Oh, my goodness, tea! Would you like some, Frank?"

"No, thank you," he said, keeping his eyes on Callum.

"I'm all right, thanks. A bit foggy."

"I'll bet. It looked worse than it was, if that makes you feel better. What on earth did you hit your head on?"

Callum slurped more of his tea. It had cooled with the window open. "The mirror. Maybe I had a few too many."

"You said that before, but the mirrors were fine, weren't they, Frank? Nothing broken except you, dear."

Instead of answering her, Frank reached for Callum. "May I?"

Callum downed the last of his tea and set the cup aside, jutting his chin forward where Frank gently turned it. Looking him over, Frank's face darkened with confusion.

"Am I all right?" Callum asked.

Frank appeared to shake off what had been bothering him, brushing Callum's jaw with the back of his cool fingers. Whether it had been intentional or not, Callum couldn't say. "Yes, I think so. Rest for today though. I'll call in a favour with Karl. We can tour the Institute tomorrow."

"Oh god, the Institute?" Anne asked. "After what's just happened? Doesn't Magnus have enough test subjects already?"

"Magnus is in Paris," Frank said, making no hurry to get up. "Karl says he may not return for some time."

"Yes, well Karl seems to be taking full advantage of the cat being away."

"Sorry, Magnus?" Callum asked.

"Magnus Hirschfield runs the Institute of Sexology with several of his most trusted partners. Karl, the young man you saw me talking to last night is his closest."

"His… closest?"

"I'm sure you understand." Frank smiled as he stood. "I've put bread and a couple of sausages in the kitchen. Try to eat something, both of you."

"*Jawhol,*" mocked Anne, saluting him from the window. "And thank you."

"It's my pleasure, and Callum?" The man gave him a stern, yet mischievous look. "Try to remember you're among friends, now."

CHAPTER FIVE

"So Frank is friends with this… Magnus, or Karl, who runs this institute for pansies?"

Anne rolled her eyes, making no effort to hide it. "You mean the place where you're sitting, where they can hear you, run for people like us? Yes, Magnus has been running it for years. He used to give the most marvellous lectures, or so I'm told. Of course, that's why he's now going all over the world with them. Karl's a bit serious, but he's sweet."

"And Frank fits into this, how? I mean obviously besides being… one of us."

"So, it's 'obvious' when it's Frank, but you get to be coy about it?"

"I wasn't coy."

"A claim I could take far more seriously without that bandage on your head. I told you to wear a hat."

"I'm fine," protested Callum.

"If you say so, darling. And you promised me you'd eat."

"I did!"

"Well, you still look positively green around the gills. Like a poster for that film, *Frankenstein!* I swear, if I unwrap that bandage, will I find stitching all around? A couple of bolts, perhaps?"

The image made Callum laugh, much as he didn't want to.

"And here they are."

Callum looked up to find Frank smiling at them.

The tall man he'd been speaking to at the Eldorado, soon introduced as Karl, stood by Frank's side and gave them a curt nod. "Welcome. We are always pleased to meet Frank's friends."

Callum muttered a hello. The man didn't seem very 'pleased' about anything.

"I'm sorry," said Anne brightly, getting to her feet. "My cousin's forgotten his manners."

"Yes, sorry. I'm Callum." He extended a hand, which Karl accepted with clear scepticism.

"Karl is the Institute's chief archivist," said Frank. "He also runs tours here."

"Until yesterday. Sadly, there has been less and less interest in supporting our work in recent times. But it continues, despite our troubles. You appear to have had some of your own?" Karl pointed to Callum's bandage.

"Oh, no, I just fell."

"In the bathroom at Suzi's. Can you believe it?" Anne chirped. "I did promise him adventure."

Karl nodded. "Perhaps you are having too much adventure."

"No such thing for Magnus, it seems," Frank said. "Paris, indeed?"

"Yes, Paris," Karl muttered. "Frank, will you join us?"

"Someone has to keep you honest," Frank joked.

Karl cracked what Callum suspected was the closest he'd get to a smile, and led them inside. Callum wasn't sure what he'd been expecting, but ten minutes in, his mind's eye was awash with photographs. Men, women, transvestites, gender-changers, and people who defied the established social order of man or woman entirely. Attractive women in well-pressed suits and top hats. Women doting over one another in the domesticity of their kitchens. Men who confidently embodied the kind of prim 'pansy' the boys back home always mocked. Some filled out fine dresses in a style that would have put most fashionable ladies to shame. Women standing proudly alongside their husbands, both dressed in fine skirts. And then, there were blokes like him. Simple looking fellows, draped around others, smiling with no care for what the world thought. He'd seen plenty of blokes dancing together in Berlin's clubs, obviously, and women too, but photographs? These were undeniable and irrevocable proof of who they were and what they could be. He'd done his best to pay attention when Karl had gone into the more detailed science and fancy names, but it had gone over a head too full of those faces.

"Amazing place, Berlin," he'd said at one point.

"Berlin?" Karl raised an eyebrow at him. "My friend, this is everywhere."

The tour continued through the Institute's research, even an operating room where Karl claimed several people had successfully altered their outward gender. It would have all felt fantastical to Callum, had the last day or two not put his wildest imaginings firmly in the realm of the possible. This, however, was no dream. This is what people like Karl and Frank were doing for real. He halted on that thought as Frank left them alone. What was Frank doing here? What did the man do at all, besides showing up at oddly ideal moments, being charming?

"Karl," Anne said. "You know how much I admire your collection, and all the work you do here, but it does bear one glaring omission."

"You'd like us to photograph you?" he asked, stifling a laugh.

"I don't see why not. Callum was just saying last night, I've a face made for the pictures, weren't you?"

It wasn't quite how Callum remembered their conversation.

"Why don't we get a picture together, darling? For the Institute's archives, or for science or something? A sort of… cousins in queerness thing."

"No, I don't think so." Callum reflexively pulled away from her.

Karl offered them another faint smile, this time seeming genuine. "Only if you wish. Unless you are afraid that people will see… in England?"

Sparks of anticipation teased his fingertips. All his life, he'd wanted to be seen for the man he was, but documented? Perhaps even a face on the poster? Would they use it for recruitment— No! That was stupid. He could no more 'recruit' anyone to their cause than he'd been recruited himself. Anne's Communist friends had a better chance co-opting him for the noble crusade of the working man. And if it would make Anne happy, he could always say that's why he'd done it.

"All right," he mumbled with hands in his pockets.

"Really?" Anne asked, seemingly shocked.

"I said 'all right,'" he said again.

"Quickly, before he changes his mind," added Karl, his tone droll. "You will want a hat, perhaps?"

Blast. The bandage.

"Here," called Frank, bringing his Hamburg into the room and putting it on Callum's head. He tilted it so that the bandage, if not entirely invisible, no longer looked like quite such a medical catastrophe. He then straightened Callum's jacket. "Quite fetching on you."

In the time it took Karl to return with the press camera, its flashlamp looming above the box like a threatening eye that could pick up every stain on Callum's clothes, Callum wondered if all 'tourists' who came through the place had the honour of such a photo, or if there were any such records of Frank, or even Max. Of course, Max didn't exist.

"Frank, draw the curtain, please."

Anne watched Frank draw the dark curtain behind them. "Should one of us be sitting down?"

"I don't think so," Karl answered, checking something on the camera. "It is better if you are side by side, as equals, yes?"

"I can see why you like these people," Callum muttered.

"Hush," Anne giggled. "Watch for the dicky bird."

"The what?" Callum just had time to look up as Karl counted down in German and the room exploded with light. He blinked away his astonishment, the entire room looking back at him in negative.

"Was that all right, or shall we do another one?"

"No need," Karl checked the camera again. "I can make you a print downstairs. Perhaps… forty-five minutes?"

"Oh, yes please! Isn't it marvellous how fast they can finish these things?" Anne grinned. "Do you know, I read they're even doing photographs in colour now?"

"Sounds a bit… bourgeois," said Callum to a polite chuckle from Frank.

"If you're going to say such horrid things, I shan't be taking you anywhere."

"Sorry."

A young man with painted green fingernails offered them coffee with no introduction, which Frank accepted on their behalf. It wasn't until Anne jokingly asked if the kitchen had any *Fleisch* that the conversation drifted to Callum's dream. Anne sat enthralled as he recounted more details.

Frank paid equally rapt attention as he sipped his coffee. "So, they were all men? And they all had scars?"

"Most of them, yes. Some bad ones, come to that."

"In Suzi's place?" Anne shook her head. "Quite the imagination you've developed, darling. "Personally, I liked the bit about the monsters eating those loathsome Brownshirts. If dreams were horses, eh?"

"I think you mean wishes." Callum had omitted the familiar identities of the 'monsters' in question. He caught Frank's dark look all the same. "Anyway, I told you it was daft."

"Aside from your injury, which would be a rather lazy ending, it would make for a compelling penny dreadful," Frank murmured. "Are those still popular in London? I suppose not."

"I wouldn't know."

"Pity. You're quite the storyteller, Callum. No offence, but I wouldn't have expected it."

Callum shrugged, sipping more of his coffee and not much liking it. "Not much to expect."

"Oh, I think there's a good deal more to you than we can see right now."

He smiled, unsure how to answer the compliment. "If you need any joining done, or fixing…"

"Not sure how they're doing without him back home," Anne added. "He's always been handy."

"Yes, yes I'm sure you are," Frank said, not taking his eyes off Callum until Karl reappeared and tapped him on the shoulder. Callum watched the two men withdraw, whispering to each other in earnest.

"You should stay a while, darling."

"Stay?" he asked.

"You're among friends. I'm sure Karl would be happy to let you explore the library. I'd join you, but it's all a bit overwhelming for me. They are scientists, after all. Frightfully intelligent but… Well, we all play our part."

Callum felt sleepy. Nauseous, even. Whatever struggles the Institute might face, lack of heat wasn't on the list. He opened his top button and tugged at his undershirt.

"Callum?" Frank asked, rejoining them. Are you all right?"

He put down his coffee. It was definitely too warm in here. Callum wanted to shed his shirtsleeves entirely. "Sorry."

"Do you need to lie down?"

He turned to where he thought Anne had been sitting and saw an empty chair. He tried to get up, and stumbled toward it. Strong hands caught him around the waist as he lost the battle to stay conscious.

*　　*　　*

"Awake…? …awake? Can you hear me? Callum?"

He could hear the voice, all right. Whether it was Frank, Karl, or some new stranger he couldn't tell. He felt worse than he had when he'd awoken with the bandage. Maybe it was the light that bore into him from a lamp just a couple of feet from his face. He made out two silhouettes that resembled Frank…

and Jacqueline. He lurched in his seat only to feel Robert's hands grab his shoulders and force him back down.

"Patience," Frank said, his voice soft and honeylike. He moved the light out of Callum's eyes, so at last they could see one another. "There's something we need to discuss."

Callum stared at Jacqueline, his skin crawling under Robert's hands. This was it, then? He had seen them kill those men and now, there would be no witnesses. Had that been what today was really about? A ploy to get him back where they could finish him off? They could bloody well… He roared as Robert held him down.

"Strong boy," the man mocked him.

"Callum, stop," Frank continued. "I mean it. You'll hurt yourself before you get any answers, and you will get them, I promise. Unfortunately, we need some first."

"Oh, you do, at that?" he barked. "Piss off with you!"

Jacqueline smiled at him. "We mean it, my dear. No harm need come of this."

"Unless you do something very silly," added Robert.

"Which I'm sure you won't."

"Murdering fuc—" He snarled again before Robert cupped a hand over his mouth and held it so firm, he couldn't even shake his head. The man's fingers gripped like the bars of an iron gate in a March wind, and they were just as cold.

Frank lifted a photograph and shone the light on it. "Your portrait, taken just this afternoon. Notice anything unusual?"

As Robert released him, Callum squinted at the figures of Anne and himself that stared back at him. Head still foggy, he struggled to make out detail. "Wrong photo."

"You'd think so, wouldn't you?" Frank answered. "But the clothes? Those are your clothes, are they not? And that is Anne, standing beside them?"

"Obviously," he muttered, admittedly confused. "So what?"

"Look harder, Callum. Look really hard at what we're seeing here. Where's your face? Your *face*, Callum? Clothes? Bandage? Hat? All accounted for, but no face."

"Maybe your fellow's not as good with photographs as he thinks," he scoffed. "It's not my fault he fouled up your—"

"Ah yes, we've seen our share of 'errors in the print.' So, just to be sure, Karl made us another." Frank took out a second photo and plopped it in front of him.

Callum's eyes went wide. Again, Anne stood beside his empty suit of clothes. And to the other side of them, a handsome soldier in an old-fashioned German uniform. His face was clean, unscarred, even proud, but Callum recognised it immediately.

Max.

"How did you…" He trailed off, shaking his head. "No, no, I'm not having this. It's a good trick though, I'll give you that."

"Would that it was. You described your 'dream' in such detail, Callum. And now, this man? Or is he an error in the print as well?"

Though he kept himself composed, Callum's heart raced. He began to understand what people meant by feeling 'butterflies' inside them. Yes, he'd mentioned Max, perhaps with enough detail that they'd recognise a photo of the man. But they hadn't just recognised one. They'd *made* one, and for what? What did they mean to do with it? What did they have over him, or hope to have over him? Hell! He pushed back his chair with a start and stood up.

"Don't," Robert said calmly.

Callum immediately sat down again, this time staying put as if he were glued or strapped to the chair. He could move his hands and head. In fact, he was perfectly comfortable. But his legs and trunk would not answer when he bade them to stand.

"We're not done, Callum," Frank continued, just as relaxed as Robert's imperative had been. "If you are what we think you are, and have made the contact we think you have, you must at least hear what we have to say."

"Where's Anne?" he snarled. "What have you bastards done with her?"

"She's at her Socialist's meeting, plotting to fight the good fight and topple the bourgeoisie," said Jacqueline.

Frank nodded. "And it will be far better for everyone if she dismisses what you've experienced as a dream. The less she knows about it, the better. That's the best way to ensure she comes to no harm."

"Also, 'bastards?'" Robert challenged him. "I'd watch my language, if I were you."

"I saw you! Those Brownshirts in the alley?"

"They won't be missed."

"Murderers! Bloody murderers is what you are!"

"'Blood' being the operative word, eh?" asked Robert. "Yes, everyone in this room knows what you saw. Though 'murder' is a dreadfully common term for it."

Had he expected them to deny it? Or had expectations long taken flight from this horror show?

"You killed those men," he murmured.

"Yes," Jacqueline admitted with cool indifference. "Does that bother you?"

"Yes! You're monsters!"

"This won't make any sense to you," said Frank, his voice warm with sympathy. "But if you knew, as we do, what those men will become, you'd have a very different understanding of that word."

"What they'll bec…" He struggled again, panic seizing his chest as his limbs refused to move. Not knowing what else to do, he began shouting. "*Help! Someone help!*"

"Stop it," muttered Robert. "I'm humiliated for you."

"Perhaps you should give us a moment," said Frank, glancing at the two devils.

"Are you sure?" asked Jacqueline.

Frank offered Callum a resigned smile. "We need to start trusting one another eventually, don't we?"

Jacqueline and Robert exchanged a look, then backed away into the darkness. Callum heard a door open and light spilled into the room.

"We'll be right outside," said Robert.

"That won't be necessary," said Frank, without turning around. "But thank you."

The door closed, leaving them together in the darkened room. Callum's chest heaved. His vigour returned. His mind flooded with questions.

"Well?" Frank asked. "Go on, if that's your wish. If you think me a monster."

"What?"

"No doubt you're a stronger man than I. The others aren't here to stop you." Frank leaned forward, arching his fingertips together. "Will you strike me? Strangle me, perhaps? Knock me unconscious? And then what? You'll just leave?"

"Are you threatening me?"

"You've seen what Jacqueline and Robert are. If we wished you harm, you wouldn't be able to stop us."

Callum folded his arms and snorted. "So, what do you 'wish' then? You want me to leave Berlin? No witnesses? Just disappear? That's not happening."

"Yes, Callum. I'm afraid that's exactly what's happening." Frank tilted his head in a way that made Callum feel like a medical specimen. "And there's not a damn thing you or any of us can do about it."

He shook his head, getting to his feet at last. "Now, you're just talking rubbish. So, if I'm not a prisoner, and if you don't mean me any harm, as you say, I am going to, as you put it, 'just leave.' No offence, Mister Bakker, but whatever this is… I'd better not see your like or those bloodsucking freaks again."

"As you wish," the man answered, striking a match and lighting a cigarette. "Though at the rate you're going, I wouldn't count on anyone being able to see your *like* for much longer."

"You are threatening me!"

"On the contrary!" Bakker shot back, standing up and levelling his dark eyes on Callum, cigarette glowing between his fingers as he advanced. "You've felt it yourself, as your skin grows just a little thinner each day. A sickly pallor here, a bout of nausea there, 'Oh my, am I supposed to be seeing that vase behind me in the mirror? I guess I imagined it.' Well, let me share an insight that might spur you to some co-operation. This is just the beginning."

"Oy, all right. I'll be going now."

"These are the early stages, Callum. It's going to get worse, and there is no cure. You'll be able to talk and make noise, just as before. Even wear clothes. Make yourself noticed if you want to cause trouble, but in the end, people will choose not to see even that. Already, you no longer show up in photographs. I'll wager we could take a hundred shots and not see an inch of your increasingly translucent flesh."

"You think what you want—"

"I don't have to 'think' about what I already know. But do you know what the worst part will be? The solitude of wandering. Losing Anne. Losing everyone you've ever loved. Then, the not knowing? Oh, yes. You'll look back so fondly on your days in Berlin and wonder what the bloody hell happened. What were those two creatures you saw kill those Nazis? What was that strange friend of Anne's trying to tell you the night you visited the Institute for Sexual Research? Hell, all you wanted when you came here was the freedom to romance and fuck as many men as you wished. Well, best get to it, Callum, because your days of romancing and fucking are sorely numbered."

"You're talking rot!"

"You're disappearing! Deny the evidence of your own eyes all you want. You're a walking vanishing act, and it will happen faster than you think. All you can do is be prepared."

"Is that so? Well thanks very much for your concern. I'll take my chances."

"You'd take the chance that it will drive you mad before you've made sense of it?"

"Look, who the hell are you?"

"Ah! At last, he asks a sensible question. I was beginning to think you were past all help and of no use to us at all."

"Of use to you?" he spat out. "That's a laugh."

"Do you want answers? About yourself and the things you've seen?" Frank snatched up the second photo from the table and held it up to the light. "About him, perhaps? Because that's all we want, Callum. We're not in the business of blackmail, nor indentured servitude. We are seekers of the truth, and I think right now, that's all you want too. After that, perhaps, we can offer you a good deal more."

He opened his mouth to shoot back some caustic reply, but none came to him.

"How's your head?" Frank asked, stubbing out his cigarette in a silver ashtray on the table.

Callum grimaced, touching the bandage. "Still hurts."

Frank called in the direction of the closed door. "Enter."

Jacqueline and Robert rejoined them, this time with a small, fastidiously dressed black woman at their side.

"Evening," Callum muttered. "Are you going to introduce us?"

"First things first."

Callum flinched as Jacqueline reached for his bandage. "What are you doing?"

"Hold still," she chided. "This won't take a moment."

"I know you don't believe us, Callum. That's perfectly fair. That disbelief is our best weapon in the modern era, after all."

"The modern era? What are you talking—*Will you stop?*"

Jacqueline took his chin in her fingers. "Hold still."

The words had been quiet, even sweet, but they hit Callum with the authority of an ancient empress that bordered on godhood. The very idea of questioning her as she stripped away more bandages seemed unfathomable. Callum's gaze landed on Robert as the last of the bandages came away. He didn't understand why, but the sight of the man, from his long auburn hair to the delicate curve of his jaw as it met his chin, to the depth of those light blue eyes, his long, elegant neck, cool alabaster skin and the slender but firm contours of a chest now exposed to the third button of his silk shirt… Callum couldn't look away.

Robert drew nearer and nearer until Callum felt the back of the man's fingers on his cheek. His lips brushed Callum's, and against all sense, Callum wanted to taste what lay beyond them. But Robert would not indulge him, instead lifting his lips to Callum's cut and pressing them there with a tenderness that belied the sarcastic demeanour he'd shown at Eldorado, not to mention the bloodied monster Callum had seen in the alley.

Callum's heart seized, but his body denied him even the slightest movement as Robert's tongue caressed his cut. A sweet, tender sensation filled him, like the first touch of a warm razor in the hands of a skilled barber. But instead of drawing blood, Robert mopped it away, a self-satisfied smile on his face as he withdrew, licking the last of his sanguine prize from the corner of his mouth.

He and Jacqueline were smiling.

"What are you?" Callum stammered. "Some kind of Dracula?"

Robert rolled his eyes while Jacqueline stifled a laugh. "That fucking Irishman."

"The term is Blood Shade," Frank explained. "Or as you might have heard it, vampire."

"A pejorative you'd do well to avoid," Robert cautioned him.

"But what just happened? Are you going to kill me now?"

"But of course! I heal the wounds of every man I intend to kill. Can't send you into the dirt looking less than immaculate now, can we? Use your brains!"

"All right, that'll do," Frank interrupted, giving Robert a look. "Callum, it's as I told you, you're far too useful to us, and that's only if you choose to be. A Blood Shade's nature goes well beyond an unusual diet. I'll let Jacqueline and Robert explain if they choose, but a Blood Shade's kiss can heal most any superficial to moderate flesh wound."

Jacqueline lowered herself until her face was level with Callum's. "Feels good, doesn't it? Frightfully useful when you need to send a companion away into the night, none the wiser for what they've just given you."

"Send them away?"

"Of course, darling. It would be terribly careless to leave a trail of dead bodies in our wake when killing them is entirely unnecessary."

"Like killing those Brownshirts was unnecessary?"

"Those brutes attacked us first, and it was fun."

"Fun?"

"We're getting a little side-tracked." Frank held his hand up to quiet Jacqueline with a soft smile. "I know you have a lot of questions, and before long, I expect you to have a great many more. But Callum, first, you need to know yourself. Blood Shades are just one variety of a vast menagerie that inhabit the night."

"In English, please?" he muttered.

"Werewolves? Witches?" Robert added, ignoring a look from the silent woman who'd joined them. "Fairies, demons, angels, goblins, gargoyles, elves, pixies, ghouls, even dragons, and any other number of creatures you've likely not heard about, from every continent and shadow of the world; they all exist, in some form. You've been living alongside them your whole life, without knowing you come from a similar bloodline."

"Bloodline? Is that right? Midlands born and bred, ye daft prick, just like my father and his."

"Many whose lineage is touched by the uncanny live their whole lives without manifesting any sort of difference, much less coming into the power you've seen Robert and Jacqueline wield," Frank added. "The power to make you do their bidding? To heal wounds with a kiss?"

"To suck the blood out of people?" he retorted. "Because if that's what I'm going to turn into, best kill me now and get it over with."

"See? You do know, don't you? You've known for years. That sense that you're not entirely there. That people don't quite see you, or that they forget you as soon as they turn away." Frank eased closer to him, eyes full with curiosity. "Blood? Not in your case, Callum. Your gift—some would say curse, if we're honest—is to disappear from mortal sight. Your flesh, your hair, your bones, there's no physical part of you that won't be rendered invisible by the time you've come into your true self. As I said, it will happen sooner than you think. I'm sure that's unpalatable to you, even frightening. But we can help ease that transition. As it happens, you can help us too."

"I'm not doing a bloody thing for you."

Frank nodded, thoughtfully. "Very well. If you'd rather go through this alone, we'll stop wasting your time."

Before Callum could move, he felt the immutable grip of Robert's hands on his shoulders again. When Jacqueline levelled her eyes on him, it felt like she could stare into his soul, as if the entire room had been swallowed by those eyes in their cold, tacit confidence. The only other thing he could see was the burning cigarette of the unknown woman, who sat off to one side of the room, watching and waiting.

"This won't hurt. Just hold still."

"Let go of me!"

"I'm afraid it's one or the other, Callum," added Frank. "Either we help one another with our respective problems, or you return to your life with no memory of meeting us, nor any of what we've discussed here. I'm sorry, but things being what they are right now, we can't risk it, even with one of our own."

"Risk it? What are you talking about?"

"You've decided that's none of your business." Frank turned to the smoking woman. "I'm sorry, Brigitte. It seems we won't be needing you tonight after all."

The woman nodded, extinguished her cigarette and got to her feet.

"Wait!" Callum felt four sets of eyes on him. "You can't... I can't just forget all this!"

"I assure you, you can," Frank said. "Robert can do it if you prefer, but you'll find we're more than capable of safely erasing ourselves from your memory. You may lose one or two other details from the past two days, but maybe that's for the best."

"No!" he barked. "Look, all right, fine! What is it you want from me? The truth!"

Jacqueline rose to her full height and smiled at Robert.

"Thank you both," Frank said to them. "I think Brigitte and I can take it from here. Callum?"

Callum watched the dark-skinned woman cross to the chair opposite him and sit down. Her gaze, which never left him, bore the same curious intelligence as Frank's. She wasn't mocking him. She was intrigued, just as Frank was. Just as Callum was. He heard the door shut behind the two vampires. Not travellers, or strangers, or simple murderers. They were actual vampires, whatever they chose to call themselves. He couldn't deny what he'd seen. "And Brigitte? Is she like them?"

"I am in the room," the woman muttered.

"Brigitte is an expert in what most would call paranormal phenomena. She comes to us after... was it four years in Savannah, or five?"

"The savanna?" asked Callum. "Africa?"

"Savannah, Georgia, in America. You think the spirits of the dead only walk the old world?" Her voice chilled him, despite the warm lilt of her American accent. "It was five years. After three in Boston, and six in New Orleans before that."

"Just answer our questions as best you can, Callum. Since you've been touched by 'the other side' as it were, Brigitte will use her abilities to fill in the gaps."

"Abilities?"

She placed a single black candle on the table between them and set it alight. Frank extinguished the lamp next to him, and sat in the remaining armchair, facing Callum.

"We're ready."

"Very good," Frank said, the light of the candle flickering across his face. "So, Callum, I have to know. What is it like to kiss a ghost?"

CHAPTER SIX

Dawn came and went. By the time Callum saw sunlight again, it was coming on dusk. Frank's questions, genial as the man was, had gone on and on, interrogating every minute detail Callum could recall about the bar where he'd met Max, and everything that had happened in the moments leading up to his finding it. Where he'd been standing. What he'd seen when it was time to depart. The clothes. The music. The distinguishing features of as many patrons as he could remember. He'd described Ferdi and the others with as much detail as he could, though Max was the only one of whom he felt absolutely certain.

It didn't seem to matter. Each time his answer wavered, the candle between them mirrored it, flitting around in the darkness. Each time it did, Brigitte was there to fill in the details with unnerving accuracy, as if possessed by an objective memory of the night itself. Beyond these interjections, however, she didn't interrupt. There was also something about Frank's calm presence that made him want to talk. In that moment, Callum felt as though he were sitting with the only two people in the world who'd believe what had happened to him. Frank in particular, seemed as interested in Callum's own gradual disappearance as he did about Max and the club.

By some better sense, he'd been conscious of the hours ticking by. But as the car now carried them toward Suzi's bar, he couldn't remember falling asleep, nor the candle going out, nor Brigitte leaving them. It was as if his day at the Institute, and the curious all-night interrogation that had followed were the dream.

The sight of Suzi's, its windows darkened by drawn curtains, shook Callum back to reality.

"You said Brigitte was meeting us?" he asked.

"I wouldn't attempt this without her," Frank answered. "Even if, based on your own helpful experience, these spirits are benign, one can never quite predict how these things will go."

He turned to Frank, eyes widening. "What's that supposed to mean?"

"It means, my friend, that Brigitte can close the veil between our world and theirs within seconds, before anything gets out of hand. It's the safest possible way of doing this. Try to relax. All will be fine."

As the car pulled up outside Suzi's and Frank disembarked, Callum realised he still didn't know the driver's name. "Thanks," he said. "I'm Callum, by the way."

The man didn't move. He just stared vacantly at the road in front of him through black sunglasses, leather-clad fingers tapping on the steering wheel. Callum at last noticed the long, sharp claws that pierced the fingertips of those gloves, and heard their harsh, quiet tap on the wheel in between the squeak of leather on leather.

"Callum? Will you give me a hand, please?"

He was out of the car faster than Frank had been. His companion lifted what looked like several canvases sealed up with metal from the car and handed them to him. Then, with his bag in one hand and a photographer's tripod in the other, he closed up the small door at the back of the car and tapped the window above it twice. The car was gone before Callum could ask any more questions.

They strode up to the door, where Frank knocked with the side of his boot.

A second later, Brigitte answered. "You're late."

"You'd have me rush, or worse, forget something?"

The woman rolled her eyes and shut the door behind them.

"How long until they know we're here?" asked Callum.

"I told you to relax," said Frank, setting his bag down with a smile. "Suzi is well aware of what we're doing, and is enjoying a night off with a generous fee for use of her establishment. She might also be in the company of a very nice young lady, but I didn't pry."

Callum looked at the skeletal frames and stands Brigitte had already set up around the bar. As the pair busied themselves setting up canvas sheets, lights, cameras, and electrical meters, it began to look more like a film set than a drinking establishment.

"You're sure you don't want help?" he asked.

"Do you know how any of this equipment works?" Brigitte's tone was kind, but dismissive.

"We appreciate the offer, Callum. But don't worry. You'll be doing the heavy lifting soon enough." Frank hoisted another stand and hung a canvas screen off of it.

Brigitte adjusted the angle of one of the lights so it bounced off the mirror behind the bar.

It seemed pointless to interrupt their work for explanations he wouldn't understand, but… "What do you mean by that?"

"Making contact," Frank answered. "You're the only flesh and blood being who to our knowledge has met these spirits."

"If that's all you need, you could come with me to the toilets right now."

"Why, Callum! Buy a fellow a drink, at least." Frank grinned, tightening a hook on one of the stands. "Passing to their side is one thing, but we need to be able to monitor you. This equipment will record an approximation of what you're seeing. A shadow, if you will. Perhaps we'll even hear them. Wouldn't that be something?"

"In theory, no mortal should be able to pass to their side." Brigitte fiddled with some radio-like instrument behind the bar. "I don't know how you managed it, but these war-dead bars are a rare enough phenomenon. We don't need to tempt fate with dumb mistakes."

"War-dead?" Callum swallowed as it clicked into place. From the scars on each and every man to Ernst's instant dislike for him as an Englishman, it made perfect sense.

Frank set up the last of the stands. "We've looked for their kind in London, Paris, and other cities in countries that sustained significant losses. Only in Berlin do the dead congregate in the way you've seen. And you, my friend, may be the only living man to have seen them, much less spoken with them."

"Why only Berlin?" he asked. "And why me?"

"Both are good questions. The first is more open to conjecture, but the Shapers—um, wizards and witches, to you—"

"Hi," Brigitte muttered as if she resented the terms.

"They found a unique energy of division running through this city like a ribbon. We don't know if it comes from the past, the future, or even local fears about what's to come. There are so many variables when one is talking about supernal energies, and just as many ways they can manifest. But it offers one explanation for why there are more shades of grey here, between life and death. Such places may well exist in Paris or London, but if they do, the veil there is too thick for the living to penetrate. As for you, my friend, I suspect it's your very nature that allows you to slip through."

"My nature?"

"As a Cloak Walker. Forgive me, that is the preferred term for what you are. As you become more of a phantom in our physical world, it's possible that you become more real in theirs."

He nodded, this at last making some sense to him. "Like... *Fleisch*."

"Exactly."

"So, I'm dying, then?"

Frank put a hand on his shoulder. "My dear fellow, improbable as it may seem now, you've only just begun to live. Are we ready, Brigitte?"

"Almost." The woman placed three glasses on the bar and poured a generous finger of scotch into each before raising one.

After toasting to success, Callum downed his drink swiftly, enjoying the burn of it down his throat, though a taste of home, it was not. "One more thing. Getting in and out of this place? That's not as easy as you seem to think. I told you about the woman in the mask? She lit me a cigarette and—"

"A psychopomp, or at least, that's Brigitte's theory. An emissary between worlds to deliver your invitation. Yet, you were able to get back a second time."

"Aye, and bloody near bashed my head in trying to get back home."

Frank acknowledged the point with a nod. "Indeed, we can't have you doing that again. Brigitte?"

The woman produced an ugly olive-green jacket from behind the bar. "Put this on. Cross to their side the same way you did before, then when you want to get back, tear the buttons off the front and throw them on the ground. We'll have you back in no time."

"Buttons? You're serious?"

"Same goes if you need us to shut down the equipment at any point," Frank added. "You've come back from this place twice already, so we don't expect major problems. But that jacket is your parachute."

It felt more uncomfortable on his shoulders than the metaphor, but Callum had never had much use for fashion. With one final check that he was ready, he parted the curtain and stepped into the tiled room. Catching a glance of himself in the mirror was a mistake. His skin seemed even thinner and more translucent than last time, and there was no blaming it on the lights. It unnerved him to see the toilet tank, however faint, behind the back of his head, its silver chain catching glints of the dim light. But it also gave him something to focus on as he watched the colour and solidity return to his face bit by bit. He didn't hear the saxophone in the bar at first. It felt so good to look like flesh again. Flesh.

Fleisch.

A man passed by him, disappearing into the cubicle. He'd arrived. Now what?

He stepped out into the bar, where a half dozen male couples embraced in a tender slow dance. He spied Ferdi, Max and the others at their table, deep in conversation, but something stopped him from joining them. *Fleisch?* The way Max had said that word. The way Ferdi had told him to leave…

He hadn't thought about not being welcomed back, nor had he discussed this with Frank, who'd been too excited by the prospect of having an agent in this world to consider whether such a man would be wanted. Indeed, he wasn't dead yet. Invited or not, this wasn't his place.

He took a seat in a darkened corner in the bar before any of the men could see him and ordered a beer. The gruff bartender complied, and Callum lifted it to his lips. The bitter, acidic smell filled his nostrils, reminding him that he couldn't drink the beer in this place, not without Max's little trick. So, he had no friends and no drink, and no idea when Frank and Brigitte would activate their equipment. He knew how to leave the place, but not what he was supposed to be doing or looking for. Maybe his presence would be enough, or maybe he'd interfered too much already, and sitting here was the best thing he could do.

"Callum?"

He couldn't hide the shame in his face as Max set a beer down beside his and sat on the neighbouring stool. "*Hallo.*"

Max smiled and touched his beer, just as he had before.

Callum lifted it to his lips and enjoyed the full, predictable taste of the strong German brew. "*Danke.*"

"*Dein Deutsch wird besser.*"

Again, he was lost. *Besser?* "Better?"

Max laughed. "*Ja. Besser.* Better."

Progress, one word at a time.

Callum took a couple more sips of his beer. Still good. What was he supposed to say to a man who spoke almost no English and whose last words to him had been filled with accusation?

"We all right, then?"

"All right?"

"Ah…" Callum wracked his brain. "Ringtug?"

Max laughed again. "*Richtig! Ja, ja, genau! Alles gut.*"

Callum nodded. He could handle the words that sounded like English, especially with Max's hand resting on his leg. "Still *Fleisch.*"

Max nodded, rubbing his thigh. *"Fleisch. Ist richtig."*

The ghost's lips again tasted of a sweetness that belied death. Maybe that's what immortality tasted like. He dismissed the gooey sentiment. Right now, he was content to draw closer to this handsome German boy, exactly the kind he'd hoped to meet in Berlin… only dead. Max had been killed, probably by a French or English bullet, perhaps fired by a man who'd fought alongside Callum's father. Or maybe… Fate had played worse tricks on him of late.

To hell with it. Max was here, with him, and he was no longer afraid. Maybe it was wrong to feel this attracted to a ghost, but what was right or normal about any of this?

"You've come back?"

Callum broke off their kiss and looked up at Ferdi, shame seeping into his heart again. "I hope that's all right."

Ferdi gave him the cautious smile of a natural-born diplomat. "Just be careful."

From the corner of his eye, Callum saw Max's head tilt forward in a 'get lost' gesture. Ferdi's expression gathered a touch of slyness before he let them be. All the same, Max cupped his hands over Callum's face, covering their next kiss from view like a confessional curtain. Callum had never felt a kiss like it. Far from a simple, crude slapping of lips and tongues, it felt as if Max had filled every spare crevice of his mouth with whatever earthly essence remained in him. The man should, to some logical corner of Callum's mind, have tasted like death, but nothing could be further from this sweet reality, which wrapped him in a warmth and safety that crept down his throat until it hugged his entire body. He'd always scoffed at talk about kisses that left people breathless, but Max's robbed him of the very function, until he at last inhaled the ghost's enticing scent. He stroked the back of his fingers over the German's shirt, allowing their tips to stray inside, brushing Max's smooth chest.

The man broke into sudden laughter.

"You all right?" Callum asked, hoping he hadn't ruined whatever magick Max had been working on him.

"*Ja, ja, alles gut.*" Max grinned.

What was the German for 'ticklish?'

Max gave Callum a light peck on the lips, then tilted Callum's head forward, gently kissing each of his eyelids. He rattled off something Callum took to be an explanation, but couldn't catch over the suddenly upbeat music that had drawn more men to the dance floor.

Ignoring his tightening pants, he just nodded his approval and smiled. "*Ist gut.*"

Max squeezed his hand and stood, pulling him toward the floor. "*Komm.*"

Damn it. He'd always been ashamed to dance back home. Even in Berlin, he'd kept looking over his shoulder, hoping the place wouldn't be raided. But what was he afraid of now? Ghost coppers? Max led him to the centre of the dance floor, ducking and weaving while ghosts danced and flitted around them in time with big band rhythms that would have been sneered right off the player back in Notts. Callum tensed, a tingling of mild electricity searing his nerves as he brushed one of the other ghosts. But it didn't seem to bother the man. Maybe he hadn't felt it at all. Maybe the only reason Callum could feel Max, as the German put his hands on Callum's shoulders and started up the same jerky movement as his contemporaries, was because Max wanted him to. At least his pants had relaxed into the festivities. Time and place, Callum. Time and place.

Three songs in, there was no escaping it. He was a terrible dancer. He'd earned several laughs from the ghosts around him, but none were ill-meant. He wondered if they knew he was alive, but even while he danced, even as the playful big band gave way to a slow tune that brought Max's body close to his and warmed his heart again, Ferdi's warning never quite left his mind. Careful, Englishman. Careful.

The music lowered some more, and Max drew even closer, again cupping Callum's face in his hands and kissing him with deep, unrestrained longing. Forget what it was like for him to kiss a ghost. What was it like for the ghost to kiss him, a living man, after all these years? The sweet scent overtook him again as their kiss broke and he buried his face in the slightly taller Max's neck, resting his head against the man's shoulder. They slow danced. Max whispered something to him in German, and Callum needed no translation as they kept moving around the floor like there was no-one else there. It took several moments for Callum to hear the shouts, moans and screams that broke through the gentle safety of the place. He looked up, beginning now to see flashes of light, breaking into the room like sudden cracks in the ceiling or walls that were gone as soon as they attacked. But each flash was an assault on his senses. The convivial smell of liquor, cigarettes, happy men, and most of all, Max, struggled against acrid smells of mud, gunpowder, and rancid, cooking meat. Some awful chemical smell too, like gas. He jumped, clutching Max tight as another flash of light came with a loud bang. Not a gun, but an explosion that set the room ablaze with light once more. He saw men scurry from the floor to shelter under tables, saw them flee, searching for doors and windows that were not there. The same men who'd been dancing alongside him and Max moments earlier were now changed and mutilated, their war wounds raw, unmasked and bloody.

Callum could smell death. A battlefield writ large within this hallowed space that had offered them safety. He jumped, almost colliding with Max as a hand, its flesh burned away almost to the bone, gripped his ankle, its owner screaming over the rat-tat-tatting of gunfire and the whistling and boom of artillery shells. This was just one of maybe a dozen men who lay screaming on the floor, foetal, prone, or ignoring their own melting flesh as they clutched a fallen comrade in even worse shape.

Max! Callum shrank back in horror as the smell of burnt flesh replaced Max's sweet scent. The man's once beautiful face was now a mess of bloodied ash and mud. It fell away as Max's legs failed him. Callum caught him under the arms just in time, panicked as Max mewled at him with a mouth full of blood. The same blood caked Callum's hands as he lifted them from Max's bullet-torn body.

He felt a hand on his shoulder, then another, the scent of death stronger still, as several of the dead soldiers surrounded him and dragged him away. He recognised the one in front of him, the sneering face unblemished, but with a shirt burned right through.

"*Fleisch,*" Ernst hissed at him, the accusation plain. "*Englisch Fleisch!*"

Callum screamed as he felt hard, cold fingers dig into his side. They pushed through his gut and reached for his heart, where they squeezed with all their deathly might. He tried to scream again, only to choke on nothing as his nerves seized. Whatever the ghost was doing to him, whoever it was, it would surely kill him if he didn't…

He clutched the buttons on his jacket, ripped them free and threw them to the floor like dice. His head landed on the cold, hard floor of Suzi's with a sharp thud.

"Callum!" Frank rushed to his side, nursing his head. "Are you hurt? No? What did you see?"

Callum's skin felt like chunks of his flesh had torn away, charred and ruined. No sooner did one pain subside than another took its place with that same awful burn. The scent of smoke, mud and death filled his nostrils. He pushed Frank away with a force that surprised them both. From the corner of his eye, he saw Brigitte tense, watching them from the bar.

"It's all right!" Frank raised a hand to caution her. "It's all right, Callum. You're back. It's just us. I'm sorry. I didn't realise the trip back would be so—"

"What the bloody hell are you playing at?" he screamed, getting to his feet. "What did you do to them?"

Frank and Brigitte stared at him, eyes wide, stunned by the outburst and accusation, until Frank, also getting to his feet, turned to his colleague. "Water, quickly. And something stronger."

"I don't need a bloody drink!" Callum roared, his voice now hoarse and dry as if he'd been breathing the smoke himself. "What did you do? What happened in there?"

"You tell us," Brigitte said, calmly passing him two glasses, one with water, the other with whiskey. "Our equipment is fried."

"Damn your equipment!"

"Callum, please," Frank implored. "What's happened?"

He drank the drinks one after the other, putting the first glass down on the bar so hard, Brigitte flinched. "They were… they were dancing. Just dancing, damn you!"

How to describe the pain he'd heard in their screams? The sight of Max in his arms, body shredded by bullets?

"All right," murmured Frank once it was clear he'd get no further answer. "We'll pack up, go back to the Institute, and talk there. There's no hurry."

"To hell with you!" Calum slammed the second glass down on the bar and stalked out into the street.

CHAPTER SEVEN

Could he go back? It was all he could think about as the U-Bahn train rattled around him on its way back to Neukölln. Could he make sure Max was all right, or at least, alive in whatever strange way that place allowed?

The entire club had been turned into a bloody, vicious battlefield. He'd watched its patrons relive their deaths, one after another to a man, no longer hiding their horrific scars.

He'd no doubt in his mind that Frank's 'experiment' was to blame. He refused to believe the horror show he'd seen was a normal part of the ghostly club's nightly program. But if that was so, then it had been he, Callum, who'd brought it upon them. He, the *Fleisch* intruder, who'd brought this into the place they'd called their sanctuary. All for the promise of a few answers? Perhaps some money? Now, he had neither. He didn't even have a way to see Max.

He slid his key into the lock and began trudging up the stairs to his apartment.

"Ah, Callum? Callum!" The shout came from somewhere above him, followed by the thudding of feet on the wooden stairs. Viktor. "I've been waiting for you. I need a favour, but don't worry, is good money in it!"

Callum was in no state to be doing anyone 'favours,' but as he reached the door of his room, which might soon be locked to him if he failed to find some cash, he decided to at least hear the man out.

Viktor beamed at him, dressed in a string-vest that showed off the muscles of the broad, hairy chest that dominated his short but athletic frame. "Do you want to make fifty marks tonight?"

"I'm not in the mood for jokes, Viktor."

"It's not a joke!" Viktor said, defensively. "A friend of mine saw you the last time he came here. He asked me, 'who is that handsome fellow?'"

"A friend?" Callum asked. "You mean a John?"

"A what?"

Callum rolled his eyes. "Not a chance."

"But I already told him you'd do it!"

"You what? Piss off with you!"

"Please, Callum? One hundred marks, then!" Viktor did sound desperate. "I promise you'll like him. He's good looking, not much older than us. He does all the work. He won't even fuck you if you don't want. You just have to relax and enjoy, then, one hundred marks! Please? Please?"

"If he's so good looking and nice, why don't you charge him a hundred marks, Viktor?"

"I… have other plans, and he wants you. The Englishman, he said, just this one time."

Callum winced, asking himself if a month's rent in advance would wash away the taste of covering for a double-booked whore. He liked Viktor, but bloody hell! After the night he'd had and what he'd seen? He remembered the smell of Ernst's charred body. He looked at his hands, where he'd cradled Max. They were clean. Perhaps it had all gone away once he'd left the place, faded like a forgotten nightmare, leaving Max and his comrades free to dance again. He couldn't take money for what he'd put them through, and he'd hate himself a lot less for whoring. Hell, there seemed barely a young German in Neukölln who hadn't traded their flesh for some extra coin.

"Fine," he said. "One hundred marks, upfront."

"*Danke!* Thank you so much, Callum! I'm sure that won't be a problem!" Viktor threw his strong arms around Callum and wrapped him in a bear hug.

Don't push it, Callum thought.

*   *   *

He'd been told to expect his client at midnight, like a cheap children's tale turned tawdry panty-dropper. Not wanting to risk his promised hundred marks, Callum had donned his tightest white undershirt, rolling up the already short sleeves to show off the muscles of his arms. He'd dropped for some press-ups and a few other exercises before getting dressed, and now lazed barefoot in the room's comfortable armchair, legs spread, a cigarette between his fingers, waiting for midnight.

Cinde-fucking-rella, he was not.

His shoulders tensed as he heard the loud bang of the front door, followed by heavy, booted footsteps. Viktor had given his client the front door key, better to avoid the prying eyes of their landlady, and it was not until the stranger reached Callum's door—indeed, he'd watched 'that beautiful English boy' disappear through it previously—that a sharp rapping of knuckles on wood replaced the footsteps.

"*Komme.*" Callum hoped he had the accent right.

In stepped a tall man in a trim, dark suit, carrying a matching overcoat. His smooth hair was slicked back with wax that made it impossible to be sure of its true colour, and a clean shave heightened his sharp cheekbones and jaw. He looked Callum up and down, first with scrutiny, then with unabashed admiration. "*Guten Abend.* I did not expect us to be speaking German."

A faint rumble in his stomach reminded Callum he hadn't had dinner. Yes, that was absolutely the reason for it, no question.

"I haven't learned much," he admitted, suddenly aware of his cigarette and stubbing it out in the ashtray he'd forgotten to empty.

His client smiled kindly. "Good. I'm not paying for us to practice German."

Callum nodded. "What... what do you want to do, then? And it's one hundred marks, up front, all right?"

The man fixed him with a side-eye that somehow made him feel even more foolish. "Viktor was right. You've never done this, have you?"

Callum couldn't deny the relief he felt at knowing Viktor hadn't painted him as a regular colleague, but still… "I know what I'm doing."

The stranger took out his wallet, peeled off three crisp notes and held them out to Callum. "One hundred and fifty. Then let's talk business, yes?"

Was he supposed to refuse the unexpected raise? Not bloody likely. The money felt crisp and clean, even as he slid it into his greasy pocket. "Right then. What do you want?"

"To see you," the man said with a smile. "To start, anyway."

It took Callum a moment to register the simple request, but he quickly peeled off his shirt and began unbuckling his trousers, wishing at once he'd chosen more flattering underwear, or none at all.

The stranger circled him, inspecting his body in every detail, brushing Callum's modest but decent musculature with his fingertips. "You play sports?"

Callum shrugged. "A bit of football."

"Ah." The man's touch strayed to the cleft of Callum's backside. "Yes, that's clear."

Callum heard the movement of cloth behind him before the man came back around front. Callum's jaw damn near fell from its joint. Viktor had said nothing about his client having abs and pectorals chiselled straight off Mount Olympus. He shivered as the man stroked his cheek with those same cold fingers.

"I like to see men enjoying themselves," the man answered. "I think you will, yes?"

"I…" An awful thought invaded Callum's brain, punctuated with memories of the Saxon beauty who'd billed him the morning after. Was this man really going to pay *him* for sex? Viktor was as hard up for money as he was. He'd heard of fairies being sold out by jealous ex-lovers and others with secrets too big to risk. Viktor would probably do it for a few lousy marks! And why, why was he doing this, after what he'd just seen? The smell of burning flesh… The thoughts shorted his brain, one after the other. "I can't."

"But you could take my one-hundred and fifty marks?"

"Here!" Callum fished them out, shaking his head. "I'm sorry."

"And we have a deal. It's not about the money."

Callum lowered his arm, breathing heavily. "What?"

"Show me your cock."

When another moment's hesitation bought him no reprieve, Callum slid his underwear down, tugging several times on the flaccid meat that sprouted from a thatch of dark, ungroomed hair, trying to animate it.

The man interrupted him. "You don't like men?"

"I do," he protested. "Sorry. It's not you."

"I know that." The man rolled his shoulders, pushing out his powerful chest as he leaned back on Callum's bed, every muscle in his arms shaming Callum with its earnest showing off. "Do you want to touch me?"

Swallowing his nerves, Callum accepted the invitation, but even the smooth flesh of the stranger's body couldn't wipe the image of Max's broken, bullet-ridden form from his mind. "I can… suck you off?"

"Perhaps we should talk instead? I think, my friend, that my body is not the most extraordinary thing you've seen during your stay in Berlin."

Feeling his throat tighten, Callum pulled his underwear back on. "I think you should leave."

"And leave you to wonder what this is really about? Why Frank Bakker and his pet abominations wanted so badly to see and understand what you saw? Bakker is a liar among liars, make no mistake."

"All right, out with you!"

The man watched Callum with perfect composure. "You're quite beautiful, Callum, at least for the moment. There's one thing Frank Bakker tells you that is absolutely true, but it's something you know already. You're disappearing. A Cloak Walker. In German, we say *Geistfleisch*, a description taken from God and bestowed on men like you. Curious. Impossible. Yet, here you are."

Realising he'd paused his trousers halfway over his knees, Callum finished putting them on, closed his belt, and sat down again in the armchair. "So? Who the hell are you, then?"

"Heinrich."

Callum turned his palms to the ceiling.

"Heinrich." The man looked as satisfied with this answer as he had with the disbelief that had frozen on Callum's face as he'd tried to pull up his trousers.

"All right, Heinrich, off with your fancy tales." He tossed the money back at his guest, who let the bills flutter to the floor with a cryptic smile. "I said piss off!"

"Without letting you consider our offer?"

Callum swallowed. "Our?"

"Tell me, Callum. If there was a cure for your condition, developed by Germany's best minds, would you take it?" Damn it. Leaning forward only emphasised the hard muscles of the man's stomach and chest. "No more dealing with Bakker?"

"I'm done dealing with him already," Callum growled. "Can't see myself being too welcome… Look, just leave, will you?"

"At Suzi's?" Heinrich finished for him. "Or do you mean the place within Suzi's, where only you can go?"

Denial pricked at his tongue, but he hesitated. Nothing Heinrich had said had been off the mark so far. The impossible body. The crisp bills he'd discarded like they were scrap.

"You said 'our' offer?" Callum asked. "Whose?"

"Patriots, who care for the future of Germany and have the resources to help you, if it's a cure you seek. You didn't think Bakker was the only man in Berlin studying the supernatural?" Heinrich leaned back again, pushing out his chest, every ripple in his muscles a power play Callum fought with every fibre of his being to ignore. "You don't have much time. Probably less than Bakker told you."

"Patriots?" Callum asked, shaking his head. "Yeah, I've seen your lot about. No thanks."

"I understand your distaste for Rohm and his thugs. But what we share is a commitment to the future of Germany. Still, I did not come to recruit you to a cause." Heinrich stood up, retrieved a small vial of clear liquid from his overcoat and held it up to the dim light. "Give me your hand."

"Never took to schnapps," Callum said with a sneer, "and I'm no friend of yours."

"Your hand, please."

If it got rid of the man faster… The cold drops vanished as soon as they hit Callum's skin. He shivered as Heinrich took hold of his wrist with a gentle, yet firm touch that testified to the man's calm strength. He lifted Callum's hand up in front of the lamp beside them, and Callum's eyes widened. His hand was no more than a shade cast over the light, except for the one small patch where his visitor had dabbed the strange brew.

"There is enough to restore your entire body, at least for a while, and if you help us with our research, we may even find a permanent solution." Heinrich sat down again, stretching his muscular arms over the headboard as he made himself comfortable on Callum's bed. "I need your help, Callum, not your loyalty. If the medicine is not enough, I can offer you something more. Perhaps something for the man you met in the place within Suzi's?"

Whatever his politics, the German had Callum's undivided attention.

CHAPTER EIGHT

Callum couldn't imagine what the surly Suzi must have thought of him, returning to her bar again, so soon, and alone. But he'd brought pfennigs and she'd poured beer, until at last, his nerves fortified, he'd gone through the curtain and emerged in the bar of the dead.

The bar within Suzi's—whatever the ghosts called it—greeted him with a slow tune accompanied by the hiss of a needle on vinyl. He'd steeled himself for what he might see, Max and Ferdi's place of refuge turned into another bloody battleground. Instead, an eerie peace pervaded the room, as two solitary men curled in each other's arms turned around the dance floor like a slow top.

He ordered yet another beer he couldn't drink, and scanned the dark room for Max. The two men on the floor ignored him, and beyond the bartender, there was no-one else to see. His pulse quickened as he considered what more could happen to a man whose violent end had already come in battle. His hand itched where Heinrich had poured the strange potion. He scratched at it, only to feel a burning under the angry red mark that had risen in its place. Then, a hand landed on his shoulder.

"Why are you here?" Ferdi asked, his once friendly voice now stern.

Callum turned to look at the man, and at Max who stood by his side. Heinrich had made him a promise. He had to at least offer it to them.

Ferdi caught his glance at Max. "He can no longer be your tourist guide."

"Ferdi," Max cautioned, but did not contradict him.

"I'm so sorry." Callum scratched again at his hand. "I don't know what happened. Truly, I don't."

"We saw and felt what happened, every part of it. This place is not for you," Ferdi continued. "You are lucky we are the first to see you here. Now go, before you bring us more hell."

"Max," Callum caught the ghost's hand as the pair turned away. A jolt of electricity shot through his arm and up to his brain. If the mark on his hand had irritated him before, it now burned like fire. He let go of Max, clutching the spot as if he could somehow make the pain stop. But his fingers felt no heat. The mark burned, but it didn't radiate.

Max and Ferdi stared at him.

"I can help you. It'll never happen again, I promise." He winced as the pain seared his hand again.

Without a word, Max lifted Callum's wrist into the light, exchanging a couple of words in German with Ferdi.

"It's nothing. Please, just hear me out." Callum cried out as another pang shot through his hand. When he looked up, the room was fuller than he had ever seen it, and every eye in the place was on him. The music fell silent, replaced by the steady whisper of a single German syllable, repeated over and over again, a serpentine hiss that filled the room as the gaunt faces of wide-eyed men edged closer.

Fleisch. Fleisch. Fleisch.

When Max squeezed his wrist, Callum didn't wait for the translation. He bolted for the curtain, not caring if he had to split his head open again to get away from the army of ghosts now advancing on him. That's exactly what they were; a fallen army of men who'd found in death the peace, community, and love denied them in life. And with Callum's help, Frank Bakker had nearly destroyed it. Strong hands too numerous to count seized his shoulders and arms, pulling him back through the curtain into the bar. Fit as he was, there was no resisting them as they dragged him out to the centre of the dance floor. He turned his head every which way, looking for Max or Ferdi, then cried out as the ghosts manhandled him to the floor. Another shot of heat ripped through his hand. When the spirits at last released him, he nursed it, barely seeing the faces above as he tried to breathe.

Fleisch.

Fleisch.

The chants grew sharper, more hostile as Callum lifted his tear-streaked face to see Ernst staring him down with contempt.

"Ärgert dich deine rechte Hand, so haue sie ab und wirf sie von dir." Ernst lifted an enormous blade high above Callum's head and brought it down in one swift chop that severed his burning hand.

He lifted the bleeding stump of his arm. Why didn't it hurt? How was he not in agony?

More rough hands, this time under his arms, dragged him to where the front door ought to be. With more shouts in German, Callum felt his entire body lifted and tossed into the street. He screamed as his weight landed hard on the mutilated arm, then looked back to see if any of the accusing mob had followed. But the front door of Suzi's was gone, along with the windows, or any other sign that behind that blank wall lay a thriving club full of daisy soldiers.

He cradled his arm, taking care not to slip on a bank of leftover snow as he staggered to his feet. Pain or no pain—its absence, perhaps not a good thing—he needed an ambulance or a hospital. *Krankenhaus*. Finally, a German word Anne had taught him would come in useful. It didn't seem as much fun as she'd promised. First, a taxi. Nollendorfplatz was only steps away and there were always cabs waiting around the Metropol.

He staggered up the street, the thought repeating over and over in his head. He should have been passing out from the pain. He ripped off part of his sleeve and fastened the torn cloth tight as it would go around the stump of his arm. He called out to two men in dark overcoats. They passed him without a look. He called again, getting no response as he neared the Metropol's glowing marquee, where a row of cabs promised him some form of help. Doing his best to hide the bloodied stump, Callum threw himself in the back of the nearest one.

"*Krankenhaus, bitte*," he said.

The driver crinkled his newspaper, continuing to read under the street light, the smoke from his cigarette wafting up toward the cab's ceiling.

"*Entschuldigung,*" Callum said, firmer this time. "*Krankenhaus?* Now, *bitte!*"

Was the fellow deaf? When Callum tapped his shoulder and got no response, he laboured himself to the next cab, then the next. Each glimmer of hope that he'd captured the driver's attention ultimately disappointed him. He couldn't be seen, felt, or heard, though he was solid enough to drag himself up the Metropol's stairs and into its lobby.

"*Hallo?*" He called to a passing usherette. "Help me, *bitte.*"

He called again, clumsily bumping his way through the swinging doors into the amphitheatre, where Buster Keaton's wide eyes and blank expression loomed over an audience of laughing Germans.

"Help!" He cried over and over, clutching his arm, trying to stem the bleeding as he made it down the aisle, looking at one face after the next. They refused to see him. He at last reached the stage, looking out over the assembled crowd. He remained unseen and unheard, except to one man in the front row. Half the flesh of his face had been ripped away, ruining one of his eyes, and he bled from an angry bullet wound at the back of his skull.

"You have scars now, Englishman," said Ferdi, his voice as cold as it had been in the club. "Like us."

"You… you mean I'm dead?" Callum sat down on the stage, letting the projection flicker above him as the audience laughed again.

Ferdi snorted a chuckle under his breath. "I did not say you were one of us; only that you have scars. Ernst can control his temper, but… perhaps making him relive his death was too much."

"What… what was that he said to me?"

"It's from the Bible." Ferdi shrugged. "The book of Matthäus, 'if thy right hand offends thee, cut it off.' Now, you know how to say it in German. I doubt you will soon forget it."

Callum cringed, shaking his head. "I'm sorry. There was this bloke… He wanted to learn—"

"I do not need your explanation."

A fresh rivulet of blood ran from the stump. "Why doesn't it hurt? Am I going to die?"

"Am I supposed to know?" Ferdi asked. "I lived. I died. I found my way here. Your path is more complicated. I don't know what you are, or what's happening to you, but it is what allowed you to visit us, yes?"

Another laugh from the audience. Ferdi's face was the only one that remained passive.

Callum swallowed. "Can I talk to Max?"

"Max does not want you to see you."

"Please? I need to—"

"Sorry, I misspoke. Max does not want you to see *him*. Outside the sanctuary, we cannot hide our scars."

"But I can't go back to the club, can I?"

"It is better that you forget Max and let him forget you. You're two pretty boys who enjoyed a few moments together in a bar. There will be others, for you at least."

"But I feel like I'm… like I'm almost not there!"

"I know. Do you want to tell me why? Perhaps I should tell you. You're disappearing, yes?" Ferdi leaned forward in his seat as the crowd's laughter and the film score grew quieter. "Why did you come to Berlin, Callum?"

"Anne. Her family's got money. She bought—"

"Do not lie to me on top of being an idiot. I asked *why*, not how." Ferdi at last stood, drifting over and resting his hands on either side of the stage, his ruined face turning Callum's stomach with the smell of charred and rotted flesh, inches from his nose. "For the boys? To feel seen by them? More than by the father whose money you stole to buy a train ticket?"

Callum was too fixed on Ferdi's injuries to deny the truth.

"Do you think you are the first? Max and I enlisted so we could be together. You became a thief and ran off to Berlin to fuck beautiful men. Neither plan worked out quite as we had hoped, did it, Callum? You're a very attractive man. So, why don't you have some new German boy on your arm night after night? Is it your lack of money, or your lack of solid flesh?"

That did it. Callum grabbed Ferdi's shirt, snarling in the ghost's ruined face. "Does this feel solid enough, you Jerry bast—"

A sickly green vapour shot from Ferdi's mouth, filling Callum's nostrils with a noxious smell that burned him from his eyes to the back of his throat. Callum fell back on the stage, clutching his face with his intact hand. Any trace of noise in the darkened cinema fell away beneath his muffled screams.

The burning grew, enveloping his neck, his shoulders and chest, down his back and stomach until it pricked its way through his buttocks and groin, reaching down his legs until it at last wrapped his feet in blistering heat. He shed his shirt and trousers, and was trying madly to peel his undershirt up over his head when he felt the touch of a cool, soft hand on his shoulder. As this new presence pulled him close, the pain fell away, replaced by the sensation of firm, supple flesh against his back as ghostly arms gripped him tighter. Callum tried to turn, to see the face of his rescuer.

"Don't," Max whispered in his ear, catching his shoulder.

Callum relaxed, recognising the voice, the touch, the odd calm he felt pushing against the man. "I thought you didn't want to see me."

"Not here."

Callum wanted to bury his face in the ghost's chest. All the questions he'd had, the offer Heinrich had made, all the things he'd wanted to say to Max fell from his mind as the ghost gripped the stump of his hand and squeezed. A faint ache shielded him from what should have been the kind of excruciating pain Max had felt the day a stream of bullets had torn through his gut. Instead of Max's soft skin, he felt cold mud and the roughness of Ferdi's overcoat before another shot carved through the back of Ferdi's head. A stray shell destroyed half his face before he too succumbed to his wounds. The foul smell of gas burned Callum's nostrils.

Max needed him to see it and feel it. They needed him to know.

The gentle warmth of a small dance hall replaced the grim battlefield. A place of fun and merriment, or so it had been in years gone by. Women smiled through blank, grey faces as children ran around them. Old men hoisted oversized mugs of beer, while a middle-aged man argued with one of the women in a manner that had to mean they were married. The only men in the place under forty were Max and Ferdi, dancing silently in the middle of the hall. The scene turned first into the rowdy, familiar sight of Suzi's… then their sanctuary. That's what Ferdi had called it. And even if he and Max's love had failed soon after, their refuge for men who'd never returned, where they could know peace away from the orders and judgements of barking, power-hungry men remained.

Even Heinrich had admitted that their knowledge of such places amounted to less than what Bakker and his cohorts knew. But the elixir he'd dripped on Callum's hand had proven his offer. If Heinrich's associates had the power to make Callum visible and solid again, what was to stop them granting Max interaction with the outside world, if only for a while? Max, Ferdi and the others could go out and reclaim just a little of what was stolen from them. What was being stolen from him now. *That* was why he could enter their place. A living ghost, welcome in a place for men stolen from their time.

Callum squeezed Max's hand, but Max did not squeeze back. It was as if in that strange, shared moment, something had changed. In accepting an invitation into Max's thoughts, he'd allowed Max just as surely into his. Heinrich's offer was on the table.

Pain from the stump of his hand stabbed through him once more. Max's hand faded with a greenish glow, stretching and wrapping around the wound, tighter and tighter. Far from bringing relief, it brought a searing heat that blanketed Callum's vision with blazing white light. When it faded, he felt Max's hand around his. The hand that had been severed, now restored, wrapped in Max's touch. Flesh on flesh, no *Geist* left between them. For the few seconds it lasted, their thoughts became one and the same. What it meant to touch one another, unharmed and visible in a world they could share.

The crowd in the Metropol laughed as Buster Keaton fell off a ladder and tore through an awning to the street below. Then, they screamed as Callum, still half-naked and blinded by the projector's light in the theatre's darkness, fell off the stage.

CHAPTER NINE

"Callum? Callum? Can you hear us?"

Frank's voice stirred him back to consciousness, followed by the stale smell of cigarettes and old books.

"You're at the Institute, my friend. You caused quite a stir at the Metropol. I had to bribe the police."

"The police? What are you—"

"Darling, you fell off the stage," chirped Anne before taking another puff of her cigarette. "What you were doing *on* stage with your pants around your ankles is anyone's guess."

He checked his hand with a start, finding to his relief a fleshy palm spouting five calloused digits, even if it did look paler than usual. He lifted his other hand. It looked exactly the same. "What's going on?"

"You're lucky one of Karl's friends at Moabit hospital noticed something off about you," answered Frank. "God knows what even the most open-minded doctor would have made of it. Anyway, you're safe. What do you remember?"

It wasn't that he trusted Frank Bakker, even with Anne by the man's side. He definitely didn't trust the people Frank called friends. Not 'people,' but monsters. Perhaps Frank was no better, but what choice did he have? He didn't try explaining *why* he'd returned to the bar. Frank didn't seem like the sort of man who liked apologies being made for him. But he managed to articulate the rest, ignoring Anne's choking as he described his dismemberment, though she perked up a bit when he mentioned Max holding him.

"It does sound like the most dynamic dream," she said. "What on earth did Suzi pour you?"

Callum shook his head. "It wasn't a dream."

"Sometimes our most vivid fears or desires can feel so real to us, it's easy to confuse the two, especially in a place like this." Frank turned to Anne before Callum could ask what he meant. "Anne, will you be a dear and tell Karl that Callum's awake and to the best of my knowledge, no worse for wear?"

As Anne sauntered from the room, Frank drew closer to Callum's ear. "Careful, there. The less your cousin knows about what you've seen, the better."

Callum frowned, easing himself up on the leather couch. "She doesn't know what kind of work you do?"

"Does she know what you are?"

On this, he couldn't argue. "She seems caught up in your business, all the same."

Frank sighed, caught in an omission. "That's more on our part than Anne's. I'll be blunt with you. Anne came into contact with the Institute shortly after moving here, as curious newcomers to Berlin of… non-traditional persuasion often do. To us, she meant no more than an acquaintance, until you arrived."

"What do you mean by that?"

"You may not have seen him, but Robert knew you weren't human the moment he picked up your scent in one of the bars. Our people report any such 'gifted' newcomers they encounter as a matter of course, but given your connection to Anne, it only made sense to foster that relationship until you could be brought into our fold."

"Where you could use me?" Callum seethed. "Watch me?"

"Protect you. And observe you, yes, in so far as we needed to confirm Robert's suspicions. The photo of you two gave us that. As for the spirits in the bar… Callum, I am truly sorry for how that turned out. I swear to you, we didn't know the apparatus would harm them."

Callum shook his head, muttering under his breath. "I didn't either." He paused, gathering his thoughts to describe the battlefield. The wounded and the dead. Max and Ferdi.

"I… truly don't know what else to say." Frank's face was heavy with shame. "As for the secrecy, you must understand, we cannot share our work with the world at large. Especially not now, in Germany."

Callum shook his head again. "I don't see what that's got to do with ghosts and ghouls."

"Politics and the paranormal? The intersections may surprise you. But again, the less you know, the less Anne knows, the safer you both are. The National Socialists may be one election away from shutting this place down. Do you have any idea what they'd do if they discovered us?"

"The… the Institute?"

"Yes, the Institute." Frank squeezed his hand. "But also, people like you, Robert and Jacqueline. In ambitious hands, even what little knowledge we've accumulated about you and your kind could bring catastrophe. I'm talking about this country's future, and Europe's. You've arrived at the wrong end of the party, Callum. But one must stay hopeful. The future is always in flux, after all."

"You're not making any sense."

Frank nodded, solemnly. "I'm glad to hear it. You'll be able to go home soon, I promise."

"Home?"

"To your rooming house. I hope you weren't planning on rushing back to England. Putting aside my own interests, I wouldn't advise it in your condition."

Before Callum could ask what that meant, he heard a familiar voice speaking in German with Karl. A tall, broad-shouldered silhouette blocked the light from the next room, where the figure stopped, acknowledging Callum with a polite nod and a smile before Karl walked him out.

Frank's eyebrows arched with more than a hint of lust. "If you know that Adonis, I do hope you'll introduce us."

Callum tried to smile, but he doubted he'd be introducing Frank to Heinrich any time soon. "No, I don't."

"With the look he gave you?" Frank shook his head, teasing a playful smile. "If you were anyone else, I'd insist you chase him down until he's at least agreed to a beer."

Callum pondered the missed opportunity without mourning it.

"I'm afraid though, that your—"

"Yeah, yeah, my 'condition.' I'm disappearing. I know that!"

"Will you please lower your voice?"

The sudden rebuke seemed so unlike Frank it took Callum back a pace. "Sorry. But can you do something about it or not?"

"Something about it? Based on our examination, it's gotten worse in the short time since we last saw you. In fact, in the time you've been in this room, I've seen a marked difference in both your colour and translucency. Frankly… Ah, you're back."

"Not for long," Anne chirped. "Brigitte's taking me skating at Busch's, or perhaps the zoo, we're undecided. All sounds so dreadfully wholesome, doesn't it? How are you feeling, darling?"

"Good," Callum lied. "Embarrassed, maybe."

"Embarrassed? A month in Berlin and you've already made your Metropol debut? Dietrich would be jealous."

Frank laughed as Brigitte joined them.

"Shall we go?" the American woman asked, taking Anne by the arm.

Anne grinned, kissing Callum on the cheek before they left. "Try to take better care of yourself. If you insist on having such a rough time, there are clubs for that sort of thing. Karl knows them."

Karl turned, his eyes shooting daggers as Brigitte whisked Anne out to the snowy street.

Callum looked at his hand again. Clear as day, he could see a vase in the next room through its evaporating flesh. "She doesn't see it, does she?"

"Jacqueline worked her wonders so that to Anne, you just look a little poorly. We thought it best she didn't grasp the full extent of your condition."

"You just do that, do you? Decide what others should and shouldn't see?"

"I don't mean to patronise you, but have you thought for a moment what would happen if all and sundry knew about what goes on in Suzi's bar? Mix up a good dose of religious hysteria with the wails of every war widow and mother who lost a son and you can forget any notion of 'rest in peace.'"

"How would anyone else even bloody get there? Even your lot couldn't reach them without me. It's this bloody disappearing act that lets me in, isn't it?"

Frank gave him a stern look. "Our instruments would have worked just as well without you. Your job was to be our eyes and ears, providing us context for those numbers. Still, from what you've said, it's a good job you were there! If Brigitte and I had taken the test to its conclusion, there's no telling what might be left of those poor spirits. We aim to study, not to harm or banish or exterminate. Take my word for it, there are others who would care a lot less."

"You're not going to try it again, are you?"

"Heavens, no! But we still need to understand the place. We have your recollections and we can speculate based on those, but without quantitatively measurable data, there's nothing to help us find or understand other, similar places."

"Is that what this is really about?" Callum asked. "You want me to come with you? Be your 'eyes and ears,' like you said?"

"I'm offering you a chance to put the inevitable to good use, not to mention find friends among the few souls who might understand you. We can offer a good wage too, if you like. What did you have planned? To go back to England and disappear? Or perhaps to stay in the bar, among the dead? To stay with this 'Max' who you've known for all of…"

Callum had already retreated into his own thoughts when he noticed Frank trail off. He tried to pretend he was paying attention.

Frank, however, was a remarkable student of human deceit. "Do you even know what that would mean? Good god, man."

"I don't know what you're on about."

"Yes, you do, and I'm telling you to get the idea out of your head this instant. They're *dead,* Callum, as animated as they might seem. Max is dead. He doesn't belong among the living and you don't belong with him."

"Oh, come off it! You said so yourself, it's not like I know him!" A lie. As Max had wrapped his energy around Callum long enough to restore his hand, he'd felt like he'd never know anyone better. "He doesn't even speak English!"

"Callum, that is *not* your biggest hurdle to domestic bliss here. Once more, they're… Oh, Callum, you're not—"

"Oh, piss off, I'm not gonna top myself! I just thought… Forget it. It's daft."

Frank took his hand and squeezed it. "You thought you'd disappear there?"

"I'm disappearing anyway. At least they can see me! Or…" Or what? As if he'd be welcome back in the bar. They'd cut his bloody hand off; the same hand Frank was holding and stroking with his thumb. Callum had never had a bloke—a living one at least—hold his hand like this before, with no come-ons or clumsy attempts to feel him up.

"I appreciate that. One of the greatest yearnings we have as human beings is to be seen for the person we are. Or more accurately, the person we want to be. In your case… well."

Frank knew. Maybe he even cared in some way. Maybe Max, in their short courtship, did too, enough to see Callum, at least.

"Are you feeling better?" Frank asked, squeezing his hand again. "This is the hand, isn't it? No pain?"

For the first time since waking, Callum smiled. "No. Did it really come off? I mean here, in the living world."

"That's a very astute question. When you manifest in the ghost realm, does that mean you also become spirit, protecting, in theory, your physical body? Honestly, Callum, we just don't know. There's certainly no scarring there now. Why your hand, in any case? Seems awfully…"

"Biblical?"

Frank frowned.

"Just something the bloke who cut me said. Some bit from the German bible. But my hand was itching like mad. Burning, almost. It's never done that before."

"So, something's changed." Frank turned his hand over and examined it like a palm reader. "Well, we can run some tests. They'll be quite painless, I promise you."

Callum wished he could hide the truth as easily as he could hide himself. He knew exactly what had changed and could have saved them the trouble. "I think I'm good."

"I'm glad to hear that, but it isn't just your welfare I'm thinking of."

"I said, I'm good. No offence, but last time you ran one of your 'tests'—"

"My friend, this will be entirely different."

"Will you stop talking this rubbish about us being friends?"

Frank's frown turned angry, if only for a moment. "I'm sorry. I suppose I just have a nasty habit of taking care of men who fall unconscious in public places."

"To keep it hushed up? Some good Samaritan, you are!"

"Fine," Bakker snapped, letting go of his hand and getting up. "No more tests. I can only offer what we've offered. For now, perhaps a good long walk?"

"A walk?" Callum muttered, slowly getting to his feet and following the man to the entrance, where the door was wide open.

Frank handed Callum a long, heavy grey coat. "It was not a suggestion. Your boots are there."

Callum angrily filled the sleeves, and pulled the front of the coat tight. He'd only just put on his boots when the door to the Institute clicked shut.

CHAPTER TEN

Callum barely noticed the cold as he trudged through the Tiergarten, avoiding the paths and so avoiding other people, not knowing or caring where he ended up. A walk? He just had to get his blood pumping. To be away from Frank and his menagerie of monsters. Away from angry spirits who'd dismember him as soon as look at him and from vague promises of visibility that only caused more trouble. Why had he even come? Just in time for winter, and a thief, no less! Lounging around Berlin sucking the cocks of desperate Germans was the luxury of a rich man, or at least, a richly educated one. Callum knew he was closer to the boys who turned their arses up for a few marks than he'd ever be to the playboy tourists who bought them drinks at the Cosy Corner or Kleist-Kasino, or even the girlish fruits in their fancy gowns that haunted the Eldorado night after night.

Had he come to Berlin to be seen, or to disappear?

"Spare a pfennig, Sir?"

Callum paused, turning to the man who'd addressed him in heavily accented but perfectly clear English. The bum sat sheltered between the barren, snow-covered twigs of two bushes, though the word 'bum' barely applied. Under the grizzle of a dark, nascent beard, a missing tooth and a day's layer of grime, sat a youth who, from his tattered, oversized clothes to his command of English, seemed more Dickens than Deutschland.

"A pfennig? Please?"

Callum was about to ask the youth how he'd guessed he was English. But questioning the boy, knowing he couldn't fulfil the paltry request, felt rude.

"*Nein, entschuldegung.*" Not knowing why he'd answered in German, Callum kept walking, passing a grove of evergreen trees and rounding another snowbank, where he heard the voice again.

"Just a pfennig, Sir? Please?"

He glared at the young man he'd passed just a moment before. He'd not circled around; that much he knew. He cursed himself for looking at the ground as if making sure.

"No," he grumbled and kept walking.

"No favours between unseen men, eh?"

Callum turned and gave the youth a hard look. "What the hell are you—"

"I thought about letting you go round a third time, or a fourth, or all evening. It seemed cruel." The young man extended a hand. "Help me up? The snow is slippery."

Callum reluctantly offered his hand. The man's face dipped beneath the brim of his hat as he got to his feet. At last, he filled out his enormous clothes, which fit perfectly on Heinrich as he regarded Callum with a satisfied grin. Callum pulled back so fast, he landed on his backside in the snow. "Just what the hell are you?"

"Someone who can make good on his offer, if you're still interested. That's more than I can say for Bakker. Thank you for your discretion, by the way. It won't soon be forgotten."

"To hell with you," Callum grumbled, getting to his feet and walking away, right into Heinrich's barrel-shaped chest. "Look, all of you just leave me be, all right? I've had enough!"

"Leave you to what? To be the disappearing man in a disappearing city in a disappearing country?"

"That's up to your lot. If you're so confident you'll win."

Heinrich laughed. "You still think I'm beholden to that Jew-loathing… what do your friends call him? Angry Chaplin? At least they're funny."

"I don't give a damn if you're a Nazi or if Bakker just pissed you off. I'm not interested!"

"Ah, see? I knew you were a smart one to pick. Bakker has never 'pissed me off' as you put it, but I am a man of interest to him. Too bad I'm completely uninterested. It's strange. I thought you understood that, yet there you were, going right back to him after—"

"Shut up, will you?" Callum snapped. "The both of you can leave me alone!"

"Do you really want to be alone?" Heinrich let Callum storm off a few paces before continuing. "You want the one thing that scares you the most?"

Callum clenched his fists as he turned. It was an empty threat. Even if Heinrich were human, which he plainly wasn't, his size and strength dwarfed Callum's. But if Callum was to rely on his bark, he'd bloody well make it count. "It doesn't scare me half as much as owing you."

A genuine admiration crossed Heinrich's face. "As I said, you're smart. You can relax, once our business is concluded."

"We've got no business, you and me."

"Pardon me," Heinrich paused, conceding this. "*If* our business proceeds through to its conclusion, we'll owe each other nothing. You can go back to your life, as visible to the naked eye as the day you were born, with no further worry of becoming a figment of your countryman's imagination. H. G. Wells, wasn't it? It would make a fine talkie."

"I've never been a big reader. Are we finished here?"

"Reader or not, you're smart enough not to trudge off through the snow toward… you don't even know, do you?" Heinrich approached him, his heavy, fashionable coat looming in their snowy, eerily silent pocket of Tiergarten. "Let me make you a simpler offer. I'll tell you how the boy who just begged you for a pfennig became the man who now offers you your most improbable desires, for they're both me, Callum. You have only to tell me what it is you want most in the world. Don't overthink it. Don't speak for yourself as a child, or as a man ten years from now, or twenty. Right now, Callum. What is it you want?"

Loathe as he was to admit it, Callum's anger had given way to intrigue. Nothing Heinrich had said was a lie. Callum wanted to know how, somewhere in the back of his brain he'd known from a first glance that Heinrich wasn't human. And how familiar the boy beggar had seemed! He'd known it then too. But what he wanted most in the world? How was he supposed to answer that?

Heinrich's coat fell from his broad shoulders into the snow, exposing pale skin stretched over taught muscle, naked except for his boots. His cheeks flushed with ruddy colour as Callum bit his lower lip and looked away.

"You've offered me that before," Callum muttered. "Are you really so full of yourself?"

Heinrich cut him off with a sharp laugh. "Let's at least be candid with each other. You *do* want this, my friend, even if it's not top of the list. Don't worry, I take no offence."

"Good for you." Callum's eyes widened as he heard footsteps approach them in the snow. He looked back at Heinrich, but the man only stared at him with that same knowing smile. Callum gestured to him to get dressed as the stranger rounded the trees.

"*Guten Tag*," Callum said quickly, hoping it would distract the intruder from the well-endowed Florentine sculpture in pale German flesh standing cavalier in the snow.

The stranger paused just long enough to look at Callum. His eyes grew wide. He shook his head, muttered something Callum couldn't make out and trudged on, the steady scrunch of his footsteps on snow fading once more.

"It's not every day an empty suit of clothes bids you good afternoon," said Heinrich. "You should have shed them, though our friend may have then decided to take them for himself. It's been hard to trust people since the great inflation."

"What are you…" Callum looked down at his apparently empty sleeves. With no gloves, he'd kept his hands in his pockets for warmth. Even he could no longer see them. "What's this?"

"You know what's happening to you. It will happen again and again until one day, you just don't reappear."

"You offered me a cure for that too. Your little sample just about—"

"Yes, yes, I know what happened to you with the spirits. Perhaps it's time to start thinking differently? There are benefits to not being seen, after all."

A chilly breeze hit Callum's throat. He wasn't sure why, but it invigorated him. He bit his lip again, then licked them as he watched Heinrich push back his shoulders, making a show of his broad chest, his sturdy body, and… other animated assets. "You're telling me that kid was you?"

"Yes. But I'll answer no more questions until you've accepted my terms. What is it you want, Callum? If you wish, you can cast off your clothes right now. We can rut like animals in the snow until your twenty odd years of pent-up English countryside lust is good and sated. No-one will see us. No-one will know."

"So, you're like me? Is that why I can see you but that bloke couldn't?"

"Callum," Heinrich wagged a cautionary finger. "Your greatest want, or we can stop wasting each other's time."

Whatever his origins, it was hard to concentrate with this enviable specimen of Germanity taunting him without a thought for either the cold or modesty. But then, Heinrich had told him not to concentrate, or to think too hard. What did he want?

"To be free." The words felt glib, but not dishonest. "Or to matter, I suppose?"

"Which is it? Do you understand what either of those things mean?"

"Look, you asked me the question and I answered it."

"With words that mean nothing to you because you can't fathom their outcome." Heinrich tilted his head as he drew near enough to stroke Callum's chin. "If it's freedom you seek, you've been granted a remarkable gift. Who is freer than the man unseen? As for longing to matter… to whom, my friend?"

No longer did Callum feel exposed alongside a man unbothered by prudish morals. On the contrary, he now welcomed Heinrich's touch. He felt the anger that had wound so tightly in his chest release. Anger, directed not at Heinrich, or even at Frank Bakker, but at himself.

"It's so simple, yet so frightening, eh?" Heinrich purred, his face now inches from Callum's. "The freedom to love unselfishly, and matter more than anything to that person. Now, I didn't read your mind, but you're not so complicated a man. I can see that's what you want."

Callum shivered when Heinrich's lips brushed his. He explored the man's cool skin with unseen fingers, letting the coat Bakker had given him fall into the snow. Not feeling the cold at all now, he began working the buttons of his shirt.

Heinrich grabbed his wrist. "Know that I cannot give you that. Pleasure? Yes, unlike any you've ever imagined. And answers? Most certainly. But not love. You understand this, yes?"

The notion of loving Heinrich had not entered his brain, even if other organs were begging him to play the part. Pleasure unlike any he'd imagined? "Answers," he whispered as Heinrich's lips brushed his again. "You promised me answers."

Heinrich nodded, slowly running his fingertips up Callum's bare chest until they stroked Callum's chin. "And I am a man of my word."

The man's strength shouldn't have surprised him, but as he mashed their lips together and pulled Callum's body tight against his, Heinrich's façade fell, revealing a being long past the threshold of ordinary. Callum threw himself against the man-creature's body, all cold forgotten as they fell back into the snow, Heinrich's powerful embrace cushioning his fall. It reminded him of being a kid with Anne, finding deep nooks and valleys in trees. There, they would tuck themselves in and pretend the tree's spirit had wrapped them up in a big hug, and was now pouring all its wisdom into their childish minds. Only Heinrich was doing it for real. Each second of his embrace offered a new image in the memory of a hungry boy, full of rage. Callum felt Heinrich's hunger, and his loss. A father? A brother? The former lost to a bomb, the latter to the same muddy, gas-soaked fields that had claimed… Callum could no longer tell if Heinrich was even German. It seemed a triviality, lost under an immeasurable void that drew yet more anger, more rage at the world.

Within the embrace, an unspeakable power and heat filled a hole in the young Heinrich's heart. Callum could feel the boy fighting, as if they now shared a mind and heart as sure as their bodies intermingled. The fight for his body would come soon enough. He heard bones cracking beneath the screams of the child whose thoughts he now shared. He felt fibrous flesh beneath tortured skin reshape itself into a being of raw power and beauty. But whose beauty? Not the child, Heinrich, to whom sex and the male body remained little more than an abstract mystery. This was a different power that made the boy's rage seem paltry, and amplified it a hundred-fold.

Callum watched as more souls perished in his mind's eye. He heard their screams and felt the blasts of weapons whose horrors defied recognition. A fire turned a room of frightened mothers and their babies to ashes. A great wave of heat and death vapourised the walls of some exotic city in the far east. Noxious fumes claimed lives in their millions, not on the battlefield, but in windowless pits designed for the purpose, and so it continued. More cities, London herself, torn apart in a firestorm that made mockery of disasters that had befallen the city in years past.

In those who did survive, Callum felt a hatred unlike any he'd known. Unlike the rage of the young Heinrich, who'd lost a father and a brother… No, it was *his* rage. He saw his own father, face shorn away by a firestorm that had peppered its remnants with shrapnel. The man who'd accepted the pleasures of Callum's mouth on his sex behind The Dancing Fox before beating him near-senseless now gurgled his own blood before the muddy wheel of a truck filled with uniformed men flattened his head into the road with a wet 'pop.' Each death, each enemy, was more satisfying than the last. Wrath borne not of a child, but of a god.

Callum sprang apart from Heinrich and scrambled away in the snow until rough trees scratched his naked back. Even then, he wanted to retreat further, to where the woods of Tiergarten could swallow him completely. He had no words for the man-creature that stood before him, mouth wet with blood that trickled down its powerful chest.

Heinrich offered him a tender smile, catching the trickle on a finger and sucking it clean. "I'll save you the question. I'm not a vampire, or a daemon, or a werewolf… but the boy? The man? I am only as They remade me."

"Who the bloody hell are 'They?'" Callum wheezed in the cold, then shivered as Heinrich pounced.

The man pinned one hand on either side of him and lowered his body with the elegance of a charmed snake until his nose was again inches from Callum's. "A creature, both one and many, with countless names. Male, female, both and neither. The fury of mortals will sustain Them for centuries to come, just as it has for thousands upon thousands of years. But not like this. Never before on a scale like this."

Callum pushed Heinrich away, allowing the big man to laugh at him as he sprawled in the snow. "You're balmy, you are!"

"Oh?" Heinrich shook his head, getting to his feet and reclaiming his coat. "But you know I'm quite sane. You felt it, did you not? Watching those men melt, crushed by your own pain? Even your father—"

"I don't want him dead! Fuck that and fuck you!"

"Callum, what is death if not life at its most raw and vulnerable? Ask Max if you don't believe me. One day, a man filled with life and so much love. The next? Such tragedy need not be the end."

"You can't bloody do it though, can you?" Callum challenged, pulling on his clothes and shoving Heinrich hard again, not caring that the man barely flinched. "Bring back the dead? I must have been out of my tiny mind believing that!"

"I did not say they could be restored to mortality. Not to the life you know, nor the one that Max and his friends knew. *Geist Fleish?* Both spirit and skin? That is your gift, not Max's. But he can walk the living world again. An army of men, returned after so many years stolen by human hatred? Immortal, beyond pain or death? The ones I serve require not their souls, only blood and fury. So will it be in the coming days, but those will pass. It will be even worse than last time, but it will pass, and what is my master to do then?"

Callum shivered again, not from the cold, but from the visions he'd seen. An army of dead men fighting an unending battle, robbed of their deaths as well as their lives. "Go to hell!"

Heinrich laughed again. The fading winter light turned him into a daemon on Earth as it scorched his skin, red as the sky. "Men will destroy one another with or without your help, Callum. With or without my help, or help from the one I serve. My master merely feeds on it, an act no more evil or malicious than a cat chasing down a rodent or a wolf stalking a deer. When your friends Robert and Jacqueline lure men to their deaths, it is a sin far more deliberate than any They require. Man will destroy man, Callum. From a shouting, drunken father to a weapon that will kill millions before they've had time to blink, it's an evil borne of humans, not monsters or gods."

"And love?" Callum challenged. "Your word, not mine! You said what I'm looking for more than anything is love. You might be right. Hell, you've probably crawled into my head and poked about 'til you're damn sure. If it costs what I just saw, you can shove your offer and your 'master' right up—"

"You resist the inevitable. I'm offering you the chance to be with Max in spite of it."

Callum tried to imagine an eternity of dancing with Max while the mortal world burned around them. Together forever and ever while it just went on, the War all over again, only this time… He turned to Heinrich, sure at last. "Do you want to know exactly where you lost me?"

Heinrich's eyes widened with playful bemusement.

"Your master… Old, are They? We talking centuries, or older than that? Are They a daemon? A god?"

"They've been called—"

"Yeah, all right, They've been called many things. So why now? Why suddenly this plan of grand and total destruction now, to extend a war you say—and I believe you on this—is inevitable? A war that'll feed Them, like it did last time. Oh, yes. Last time. The *Great* War. 'The war to end all wars.' Tell me what that means for a monster who feeds on anger. A feast They're scared of never repeating? A fix They'll never find again? Not with my help, you bastard. Do your own dirty business."

"You deny yourself the freedom of truth? Your own happiness?" Heinrich allowed Callum to walk away in silence, waiting until he was almost past the trees before calling him again. "What about Anne?"

"You leave her alone!" Callum didn't care who heard as he turned and advanced on Heinrich again. "You lay a bloody finger on her and I'll—"

"There's no need." Heinrich calmly pointed to a spot behind Callum, where Anne's blue hat lay in the snow. "But if she means so much to you, you should hurry."

Callum clenched his fists, fighting the temptation to slam one into Heinrich's smug, square jaw. The bastard would only thrash him in return, or disappear, or break his arm, or worse. "Where is she?"

"Power-hungry men need armies." Heinrich pulled his coat tight around him and took his leave. "As I said, Callum, you're smart. Figure it out."

Callum swallowed, his naked fingers numbing in the twilight winter air. He knew exactly where he'd find Anne.

Shit.

CHAPTER ELEVEN

The door to Suzi's was shut tight, which didn't surprise him for six o'clock. This was a place for midnight meetings, not casual daytime gatherings. It certainly wasn't the place one expected to see a bloke in a long brown overcoat looking fervently up and down Kleiststrasse. The young tough lit a cigarette, then stalked off toward Kleist-Kasino, making a poor show of cool composure, just in case the outline of a revolver in his pocket didn't give the game away. Callum didn't know why he bothered. Brownshirts weren't an unusual sighting in the queer clubs, but they had to be rare enough at Suzi's.

What to make of that, then? Had they sent a scout out looking for him? Not unless Heinrich had tipped them off, which made every bit of sense from that slimy bastard. Callum looked at his hands again. They were faint, but he could see them. Perhaps he would be harder to see by the light of day. Or perhaps he was only visible after nightfall now—one of the ghosts, indeed!

His hands were also shaking. Invisible or not, he was not about to burst into a lesbian bar overrun by Nazis with no plan beyond scaring the wits out of them and hoping for the best.

Besides, he was sure more than a few of them would be nursing black eyes and other injuries of their own. Anne and Suzi—and the American witch, Brigitte, if she was in there—hardly seemed the sort to play damsels in distress. He had time to be clever about this. He could wait the scout out, then covertly follow him back in, assuming he couldn't be seen… which of course he bloody could! Could he jump the bloke and steal his uniform? Even more daft. Think!

He jumped as a loud pop went off up the street near the Metropol. Callum spun to see a bright flash of light, followed by the proprietor of a news stand chasing three boys up the street. In front of Suzi's, another one of the Brownshirts had stepped out to see what the fuss was about, which made Callum wonder if it was time for a little fuss of his own. Callum intercepted the slowest of the boys as the trio ran past him. As his friends beat a hasty retreat, the kid, ruddy cheeked in the cold and no more than nine years old, twisted and writhed in Callum's grip. The old proprietor soon caught up to them, spouting off an angry slew of German.

"*Entschuldegung,*" Callum got out, trying to placate the man with an outstretched hand. "He's my son. Son? Boy? *Kinder?*"

The shopkeeper stared at him, confused, even as the boy stopped writhing.

"*Ist mein Vater!*" the boy snapped sulkily, twisting out of Callum's grip and folding his arms, knowing he'd found an accomplice.

"*Ja. Ich ist…*" Knowing that less German would make for a better play, Callum leaned down and shook the boy gently by the shoulders. "Did you steal from this man? Did you?"

Whether he understood or not, the boy shook his head vehemently, then pointed in the direction his friends had gone. This produced another snarl from the shopkeeper, which Callum placated with a shake of his head. With one final curse, the man stalked off back to his shop.

Once they were alone, the boy looked up at Callum and grinned. "*Vielen danke!*"

Before he could run off again, Callum stopped him and held out his hand. With some reluctance, the boy handed over the firecracker Callum had felt concealed in his coat. When the boy went to run off again, Callum coughed, getting a box of matches for his intuition. Now, the kid could leave.

It wasn't the subtlest diversion, but as long as Anne had the good sense to duck...

Callum had heard about Silvester, the night Germans all over the country celebrated New Years' Eve by drinking themselves silly and letting off fireworks that prioritised sensation over safety. The tradition, so Anne had said, had slowed after the war, as more Germans sought neither to waste limited funds nor be reminded of their country's bloody, crippling humiliation. So be it. Tonight, Callum would celebrate an early Silvester in the most obnoxious and arguably most dangerous way possible. Damn! What if the ghosts sensed what was going on? What memories of the battlefield could this diversion stir up? He would just have to hope his little show stayed in the mortal world. He only needed a few seconds.

The matches caught with surprising ease, as did... Callum's heart caught in his throat as he recognised the explosive as a basket bomb. He pondered—in the few seconds between throwing a rock to break Suzi's window and throwing the firework in after it—what a stray spark or a resultant fire could do near a fully stocked bar. But his gift was avoiding sight, not foresight, and he'd already committed to the plan.

The eruption was loud and strong, accompanied by the cracking of wood, the whistling of peripheral sparks and the shouts of frightened Nazis. Black smoke rose from the broken window, followed by more from the front door as one of the men threw it open.

Callum covered his nose and dove inside as the Brownshirts tried to extinguish the small fires that had broken out across three tables mercifully far from the bar. If anyone had seen him, they didn't show it. This included Anne, Suzi, and Brigitte, who sat at tables in three different parts of the room, guarded by three gigantic but committed Brownshirts, who'd kept their posts through the whole kerfuffle. For better or worse, Callum was inside. He hoped the dark would shield him, or quicken his translucency or… something!

Not that approaching Anne without an apparent face or hands was the best plan either. Bloody hell!

The thug guarding Suzi shouted something at her, getting an eye-roll in response. Suzi had a black eye. The man had one also, with a cut, swollen lip to match. How did these men plan to find their way into a ghost nightclub when they lacked the good sense to not fuck with a lesbian bartender?

As the smoke cleared and the last fires were stomped out, three of the Nazis ran out onto the street, unaware the perpetrator was watching them from behind a long curtain that concealed a private table. He checked his hands again. Faded, but not gone. Come on! Either disappear or don't, damn you!

He cast his gaze around the room, counting five remaining men. That made nine of the bastards… not impossible odds if what Suzi had dealt out to her guard was any indication, but not odds he cared to test, either. Step one, down. What the hell was he supposed to do now? He cursed silently as the three men returned. So much for his advantage. He looked again at his hands. They were opaque, but not invisible. He couldn't believe he was wishing this shit would go faster.

The man who'd left the bar before his firework stunt returned with a plump, balding man at his side, one whose face dripped with arrogance beneath his spectacles. Rohm, the creep who'd had his arms around the two men at Eldorado, before they'd become food for Jacqueline and Robert. Callum cursed himself for not calling them. Had he been afraid of their monstrous power and appetites? Not half as afraid as he'd been of Heinrich's threat. It had sent him straight to the bar, and it was too late to go get help now.

Rohm weaved through his gang of toughs until he reached Brigitte. Anne shouted something at them in German, but the men ignored it. Anne, never one for being ignored, continued, earning a slap for her troubles which she repaid with a solid stomp on the attacker's foot. The Nazi spewed a furious barrage of German back at her, only to be silenced by his impatient superior. Callum knew Anne's only use to them was as bait. It didn't matter if what they had planned was Heinrich's scheme or Hitler's. He needed to get Anne, Brigitte, and Suzi out of there, *now.*

Rohm's earnest conversation with Brigitte was too low for Callum to hear, but he could add two and two. They wanted access to Max and his friends. An army of invincible, ghostly soldiers, ever renewable. Casualties? What casualties? They were already dead! And if the Brownshirts could not enter Max's world, they would bring its fallen soldiers into this one. Brigitte was the expertise, Anne was the bait, and he was the key. Suzi was collateral damage, which didn't bode well for her if Callum didn't do something soon.

"Max," he whispered, not knowing if it would do a damn bit of good. He'd never, after all, seen Max manifest on the living side of Suzi's bar. "Max, answer me, please."

Rohm touched Brigitte's jaw, but the American kept her cool until he withdrew it and conferred with the lieutenant who'd fetched him. Callum tensed as the subordinate's muscles flexed in his brown uniform. The man was no Heinrich, but any fight he picked with Callum would be over quickly, with Callum on the losing side.

Callum jumped as a loud *clunk* broke the silence behind him. He turned to see a candlestick roll away on the floor after hitting the wooden table… a candlestick he couldn't possibly have bumped.

The lieutenant stalked toward the curtains that guarded his refuge. Callum froze as the man pushed them open and looked right at him, his broad chest blocking Callum's view of the rest of the room. Callum braced himself for the man to grab his collar or worse, and drag him out. But the brute just stood there, confusion crossing his deep brown eyes as they bore into Callum.

The lieutenant's comrades called to him, until the man brought down a meaty fist to haul his prey into the bar. Callum twisted and writhed, but the Nazi's grip was firm. He heard Anne cry out, but this was hardly the time to explain why she could see straight through every inch of his exposed skin, as she surely could. The brute handling him exchanged more remarks in German with his superior, though his soft tone belied the violence with which he'd grabbed Callum. There was no throwing Callum against a table or a wall either. The man just held him firm, speaking matter-of-factly with his commander.

Before Callum could demand an explanation, the fellow yanked the back of his collar and forced him toward the toilets, his gateway to the bar that sheltered Max, Ferdi, and all the others. A lack of English could only mean they didn't need Callum's cooperation, just his presence. Suzi watched in horror. Anne objected in strenuous German, in between begging him in English to tell her he was all right.

"I'm fine!" he called several times as the brute continued manhandling him. Was he fine? Would Max be fine? Could he take this muscular bastard down once they were behind the curtain and improve his odds, just a little?

Only Brigitte remained silent, watching them… until she smiled.

The German shoved him through the curtain and into the area next to the sink. The man closed the curtain behind him, his once hard face now filled with concern. "*Alles gut?*" he asked, putting his hands on Callum's biceps and squeezing gently. "*Callum, ist mich. Alles gut?*"

"Max?" Callum fairly breathed, at last recognising the kindness that had usurped the Nazi's face. "Oh my God! They're…"

"*Ja, ja,* I know." Max breathed steadily in his new fleshy suit as their lack of a common language again stifled communication.

Callum wished he knew more—

Max pulled Callum close and took him in a long, deep kiss as if he'd been in command of this thug's form his whole life. Strange as it felt to him, Callum didn't resist, allowing Max to draw them both deeper.

"*Ist Fleisch?*" Max grinned at Callum when they at last broke.

Callum grinned back. "*Ja, ist Fleisch. Geist Fleisch.*"

Max laughed, holding him again and burying his face in Callum's neck. "*Mein Geist Fleisch.*"

The warm music and gaiety of the sanctuary crept through the curtain. As silently as ever, they passed the veil between the living and the dead.

Max's borrowed lips brushed Callum's again. "*Komme.*" As abruptly as he'd pulled Callum from his hiding place, Max pulled Callum through the curtain again, to where Ferdi, Frank, Johann, and an anxious-looking Ernst hovered around the corner of the bar. All greeted him with smiles, except for Ernst who grabbed the hand he'd cut from Callum's body— or perhaps his spirit body—and, satisfied it was restored, threw his arms around Callum's neck and hugged him.

"*Tut mir Leid,*" Ernst said. "*Tut mir Leid,* English."

Callum didn't understand, but he took the hug anyway. "*Tut mir Leid,*" he said back.

The rest of the men gathered round, squeezing his shoulders and laughing as Max vacated the shell of the living Nazi's body and joined them.

Callum watched the mortal man shudder as Max's spirit left him. The fellow looked around the bar, eyes wide, as if for all his commander's scheming and boasting, he'd not actually believed it possible. Then, his eyes grew wider, the flesh around them reddening. He screamed as flames burst from every orifice, melting his brown eyes and singeing his skin, consuming flesh, hair, muscle, bone and clothing alike until a pile of glowing ashes scorched the floor where the man had stood.

Spying the mess, the bartender launched a furious barrage of German at Max, who alongside his friends—and Callum— stared at the puddle of charred carnage, lost for words.

"Does that always…" Callum began. "I mean, is he…?"

Ferdi shook his head before putting a hand on Max's shoulder and muttering something to him in German. Absolution for bringing the poor devil to such a grisly end?

Callum tried not to overthink it. Pretending he had not just seen a man incinerated from the inside, he turned to the bartender, ready to order the strongest drink available. In some way, it made a sort of horrible sense. The beer in this place had burned him on the first sip, before Max's intervention. The spot on his hand had burned here too, thanks to Heinrich's 'cure' for his condition. But for the grace of his slow disappearing act, he might have met the same fate as the Brownshirt.

The earnest conversation between the German ghosts filled him briefly with hope, but the exasperated look on Max's face was draining it fast. He didn't understand a word, but whatever Max was trying to tell them, his friends obviously weren't going for it.

At last, Ferdi broke off silently from the group and approached Callum. "You bring us more mortal trouble?"

His words weren't angry, or even accusatory, but Ferdi's sadness was beyond evident.

"No!" Callum protested. "They want to capture you! Put you back among the living and use you for God knows—"

"Max told us what they want," Ferdi answered flatly. "But these are not your people? Strange. One of their minds feels the same."

"They're not the same!" He remembered Brigitte. "I mean, yes, one of them is, but they're making her do it. These blokes are evil!"

"Like they told us the English and the French were in 1914? Still, I suspect you are right. Life by the sword, eh?" Ferdi tilted his head at the scorch mark on the floor. "I could feel the rage in him before he died. His spirit will find no sanctuary here."

"Then, you'll help us?"

"Help who?" Ferdi signalled the bartender for another drink. "Another unseen master who wants us to fight his battles? I think not. If they try to take us from this place, they will meet a resistance greater than any you have seen us give so far. Thank you for the warning, my friend. We will take care of each other, as we always have."

"But what about Anne?" he protested. "You might not care about her, but I do. They'll... I don't know what they'll do to her if this doesn't work."

"If it doesn't work?" Ferdi asked, taking his drink and sipping it. "Then, you want it to work?"

Callum paused. He'd not looked at it that way. Or thought about what could happen if Ferdi and the others crossed over of their own free will, or were brought over by the force of Brigitte's power, assuming she could do it. He hadn't thought about any of it.

"You need to choose a side, Callum," Ferdi said at last. "I've chosen mine."

Max shook his head ruefully at Callum. Whatever he'd tried to talk the group into, he'd failed, and they were running out of time.

Damn it, not good enough!

Callum took Max by the arm and pulled him away. "Anne," he said, not caring if he sounded like a madman, or if the German could understand him. "We've got to help Anne."

Max clasped Callum's hands, casting another look at Ferdi and the others as they retreated to their usual table. He shook his head, turned back to Callum, and squeezed. "Wait."

Before he could ask what Max meant, Callum felt himself vibrating from head to toe. He felt like he was about to vomit, which in this place, on a mostly empty stomach, more likely meant blood than bile. The sight of young men enjoying a night of revelry and dancing in each other's arms faded, replaced by grim Brownshirts in all their performative bravado, their sleeves encircled by the red and white bands and broken black cross of their ideology. He was back in the world of the living, and Max was nowhere to be seen.

For a moment, the Nazis, the women, and Callum just stared at each other, awed by Callum's sudden reappearance.

If the men had doubted the existence of a hidden ghost bar before, they didn't now.

Without a word, the man guarding Brigitte pulled out his revolver and shot the fellow next to him clean through the head. A spattering of gore hit Suzi's floor seconds before the thug's body collapsed after it. The other Brownshirts stared, dumbstruck.

Max! Having possessed the shooter, Max took aim at the one guarding Anne and put a bullet in the man's shoulder, before three shots from another man standing by the bar took his mortal host down.

Brigitte, meanwhile, had dived beneath the nearest table, while Anne and Suzi had each incapacitated their captors with solid elbows to the groin that granted them precious seconds to escape. One man fired several shots at them as they found cover behind the bar. Callum, meanwhile, took shelter behind a table. He saw a bullet graze Brigitte's shoulder.

"*Nein!*" shouted Rohm, grabbing the wrist of the man who'd injured Brigitte and snatching the gun from him. More furious shouts followed as Rohm tried to get his remaining men under control, his piggish nostrils flaring. He needed Brigitte and Callum alive, at least.

A loud crash announced the breaking of the lock on the front door. Robert's auburn hair glowed in the streetlight as he surveyed the chaos. Without warning, several of the Brownshirts raised their guns and fired, plugging Robert's body with four fresh wounds. Robert frowned at his ruined shirt and closed the door behind him as the humans watched in horror. When one at last shouted at him, Robert barely seemed to pay attention.

"I came down here tonight to fuck men and kill Nazis," Robert said, taking in the room. "And I don't see any men."

The bloody chaos of shots accompanied the smell of gunpowder mingled with fresh blood, liquor from bottles shattered by stray bullets and raw panic. Every instinct told Callum to get as far from the place as possible, but not without Anne. He cast a glance at Brigitte, who clutched her arm in the relative safety of her hiding spot. She nodded toward the bar, mouthing 'GO' as Callum charged past two wiry Brownshirts like a rugby player. As he neared the bar and moved to vault it, an unseen force—Robert, he guessed—aided his momentum, then was gone just as fast. Anne and Suzi scrambled to his side as he hit the floor, ducking a shower of glass and liquor from another broken bottle.

"Callum," Anne breathed, catching his translucent hand in hers. "What's happened to you?"

He shook his head, vehemently, hoping it could still be seen. "We need to get out. On three!"

Suzi muttered something that sounded an awful lot like 'fuck three' before leading them to a curtain just four feet high. She pulled it back to reveal a small door.

"Wait," Callum looked back at Brigitte. But the witch had already thrown open the front door and disappeared into the night.

Robert slammed the door after her and skewered Rohm's beady eyes with talon-like fingers that went right through his spectacles. The man gave one last scream before Robert took hold of his overgrown throat and tore it open, tossing the entrails to the floor. Robert then dived on the throat of another terrified Nazi, whose gut exploded with bullets as one of his comrades tried to shoot the creature that was quickly turning their unit into *Weisswurst*. Following Suzi and Anne, Callum left their shouts and screams, along with the scents of blood, gunfire and death behind. As they emerged into a grimy, empty storeroom and then the snowy alley behind the bar, Callum hoped the bloody scene hadn't manifested for the spirits. Either way, Max and his comrades would be safe enough, for now.

Suzi engaged Anne in a slew of furious German as Anne, in English, implored Callum to explain what was going on. As if he had answers that would make any sense to her! He heard the words *die Grüner* several times from Suzi, which Anne clumsily translated for him as slang for 'police.' Police? Not bloody likely! With what Suzi and Anne had just seen, could he take them to Frank? To the Institute? Hell, if not there, where?

"Come on!" At least on the street they could hail a cab, though probably not one whose driver was used to men literally fading before their eyes.

"Darling, what's going on?" Anne asked again. "Callum! What's happening to you? I can't—"

"We have to go! I'll explain when we get there."

"Where?"

They jumped as a figure in a dark coat appeared before them, his pale face streaked with blood as he sucked yet more of it from his fingers with orgasmic relish.

"Mmmm," Robert moaned. "Waste not."

Suzi and Anne backed away, eyes wide at the sight of the creature licking blood from its claws in the guise of man as handsome as any about town… except for his clothes, now drenched with Nazi gore.

Robert's smile made it clear he was enjoying the theatrics as much as the flavour. "Frank needs you, now."

"Me?" Callum asked.

"Your unique skill set, anyway." Robert pointed to Callum's disappeared hand. "You can hide your clothes in the alley, there. I'll see that your friends get home safe."

As Robert put a hand on each of Anne and Suzi's shoulders, the two women stood entranced, like they'd been placed under some serene spell, which may have been more accurate than Callum wanted to admit.

"I'll take them," Callum said. "You go help Frank."

"Didn't you hear me? I said Frank needs you. I can obfuscate myself to some extent. But you, Englishman, were born to it. The man currently holding Frank hostage is also an acquaintance of yours."

Heinrich. Callum cursed his own stupidity. "All right."

"Do you want to say goodbye?" Robert asked. "I doubt she'll remember, but just in case."

If Anne saw him, she didn't show it, which was probably for the best. 'Saw him?' A grim sort of joke. He kissed her cheek and squeezed her hand anyway. "I'll see you soon."

Callum stripped off his clothes, the cold no longer bothering him as he followed Robert and the women. They hailed a taxi, where Robert instructed Callum to get in before giving the driver strict directions to Anne's apartment in

Kreuzberg, via the Institute on the edge of Tiergarten. The driver didn't question the odd routing, even when his door opened, then closed without remark as he completed the detour. Callum stared up at the house, letting the cool snow melt on his shoulders. Realising how suspicious it probably looked, he brushed it off, giving his hair a good shake to be sure. He then turned up more of the snow to obscure his footprints. He still had so much to learn.

He circled two thirds of the way around the Institute before finding an open window. What did he owe Frank, or Robert for that matter? His life?

He heard tires scrunch through snow, the stilling of a truck's engine and the slamming of its door, before an exchange in brutish-sounding German suggested his task was about to get a lot more complicated, and that Frank would need his help more than ever.

He grunted under his breath. Here the fuck went nothing.

CHAPTER TWELVE

Callum rolled over the window sill, wincing as he landed hard on his shoulder. The loud bump caught the attention of the young man with green-painted fingernails, who glanced at him, but said nothing. Callum lifted his hands up in front of his face and saw right through them. He was gone, at least for now, without so much as a shadow to give him away. He jumped at the sound of hammering on the front door.

The green-fingernailed scholar swiftly opened it and scurried out of the way, allowing the Brownshirts to spill inside. Like starved dogs they stalked from room to room, tearing books off shelves, ripping papers from desks and walls, barking orders and jibes at one another and looking for 'deviants.'

Callum gasped as something sharp jabbed his shoulder. He watched green fingernails drop silently out the very window that had granted him access. The mad bastard had stuck him with something, but what? And why?

Callum counted seven Nazis. But the casual way with which the man had let them in, the way he'd quietly slipped out, and the absence of the Institute's other associates… They'd known this was coming, and faced with a fight they could not win, had slipped out to fight another day.

In that case, where was Frank?

At no time had Callum actually seen a point—assuming there was one—where the Institute ended and Frank's domain of monster studies began. Nor could he simply walk through walls and find out. *Geist Fleisch* or not, he was still very much *Fleisch*. He dove out of the way as one of the Nazis pushed a bundle of books off its shelf onto the floor. It was only a matter of time until one of these twats swatted or tripped over or threw something at him that would give him away, assuming his gift didn't fail him first. For now, at least, they couldn't see him. But the way they stalked through the halls, tearing the place apart… He had to find Frank before they did. He needed a way to search quicker than *Fleisch* would let him. Could he call to Max, somehow? The ghost was not his to command, yet the name found his lips like a subconscious incantation.

"*Hier,*" came a whisper behind him.

He turned in time to see Max flinch, unable to hide his awful scars outside the club. But Callum would not look away. Not now. As they spent the next moment staring at each other, ignoring the chaos that surrounded them, he knew Max could see him too.

"*Du brauchst mich?*"

Their language barrier on the other hand…

Callum considered what he needed Max to do. To float through every room in the place, through walls and cupboards in search of a secret panel or opening? Or to the basement or the butler's fucking pantry in search of an endangered Frank, while Callum sat idle, waiting and hoping?

Great bloody plan, fool!

"*Hilfe?*" Max clarified, pointing to himself, then Callum. "I help you?"

It was a lousy time for a German lesson, but yes, Callum would take all the *Hilfe* he could get. Before he could object, Max's scarred face shot toward him, stretching and opening its mouth until it wrapped around Callum's. He couldn't breathe. He could no longer move, or scream. He could only wait as Max's spectral form entered him through every opening, crack and pore. His heart seized. His stomach lurched. He wanted to vomit, choke, piss himself and beat the ground with his fists all at once, and every inch of his body felt like it weighed twice as much. But as Callum staggered to his feet, the feeling faded. He still felt solid, but the intrusion no longer weighed him down. Instead, it invigorated him. He felt its familiar warmth spread through his body, sending pins and needles through to his fingers and toes.

Don't resist me. The words were in English, but the voice was all Max.

Callum went limp, allowing Max to barrel down on the first Brownshirt. The man cried out as Callum's unseen form slammed into him like a rugby player, pushing him to the ground. Callum's right fist cracked hard across the target's face, breaking the man's nose with a punch that left him out cold.

In an instant, Max had Callum back on his feet and was charging toward a Brownshirt who'd begun tearing books from one of the shelves only to get distracted by one of the pages. Callum's hand cupped the back of the man's head and slammed it into the wooden shelf. The Nazi collapsed among the books he'd scattered on the floor, limp fingers still wrapped around the volume that had caught his eye. One of the fallen man's comrades knelt to check his pulse, and got an unseen kick to the face for his concern.

"Ah!" Callum gasped as the blow jarred through his bare foot and leg. "Careful!"

Shhhh!!!

But the kick's recipient had already heard the English word. Clutching his face, he barked the alarm to the remaining Brownshirts. Every man in the place spun to face Callum. Another solid kick to the Nazi's face laid him out next to his comrade, but the other four were already closing fast.

Callum knew that to stay still would be his undoing. He went limp again, allowing Max to weave him through the men like an agile puppet. While their leader quickly dismissed several shouts of *Geist,* the Nazis stalked from room to room, searching for the *Englisch* spy. Now, Callum understood. What was he, if not the perfect spy? That was, if he could keep his bloody mouth shut.

Callum jumped as his leg clipped one of the Nazis. The man spun around, eyes wide like he'd just… no, the man *had* just felt a ghost. Max slammed Callum's fist into the thug's temple, then threw him headfirst into the wall. Another Brownshirt on the floor and three more to go. They scurried out of the way before one of the other men could corner them. This wasn't helping him find Frank!

"*Spiegel! Spiegel!*" barked one of the remaining Germans, a soft-faced youth of no more than twenty.

Callum looked in the direction the boy was pointing in, watching his own eyes widen in horror as the mirror on the wall betrayed him. There he was, exposed in every sense, a faint green glow around his eyes and neck that might have revealed Max to the knowing eye.

The ghost left him no time for doubt, grabbing the bearded Brownshirt nearest them and throwing him with all their might into the glass. It shattered, showering the man in shards as he fell to the floor, covering his face. The kid who'd called them out snatched up one of the splinters and swung it through the air, clumsily at first, then with more deliberate strokes as his frightened gaze darted over the floor, looking for Callum's reflection in the shattered mirror.

Clever bastard.

Callum cried out as the solid **thunk** of a heavy truncheon sent a shock through his right shoulder.

"*Hier!*" the ringleader who'd wielded it ordered.

Max quickly pulled Callum clear of another swipe from the kid. They caught his arm and pulled him into a solid punch that sent him reeling, clutching his face. The glass shard fell to the floor. The commander, who could have matched Heinrich for stature and musculature, barrelled down on them again. Max spun them out of the way, grabbing one of the larger glass shards as they went. The attacker aimed a solid kick at the moving shard, only for Max to catch his foot, straighten his leg, and plunge the glass deep into the beefy muscle of the man's thigh.

The Nazi's scream drowned out Callum's gasp as Max ripped the glass splinter up the man's leg, tearing a deep gash before plunging the crude weapon into the brute's neck.

Callum lifted the shard, at last seeing the blood on his now gory outline.

The kid peered through fingers that cradled his bleeding face. He went to stammer something, then when words failed him, fled towards the front door.

"That's right, fuck off home!" Callum barked. "Go on, get!" A final lunge yielded a startled cry as he sliced through the kid's sleeve. The bloodied red armband sank to the floor like a popped balloon.

They'd killed a man. Callum could no longer feel Max. He could only feel warm blood from the dead commander pooling around his bare feet. He looked around the room at the beaten and broken Nazis, wondering how many of them had shared their leader's fate. It may not have been Max's first time killing, but it was Callum's. Unless he counted complicity; the man Max had possessed at the bar, for instance, or the men Robert had killed while Callum watched.

Life by the sword. Is that what his life was to be, then?

The breaking of the mirror had left a small hole in the wall behind it, too deliberate and perfect to have been a casualty of his battle. A green glow came from inside, the same odd shade of green that had surrounded his reflection in the glass. There also came an odd, low hum that was neither nature nor machine. It soon altered pitch, until it sounded like air being sucked from the room. A week prior, he would most certainly have left it well alone. Now, with his mind awakened to a multitude of possibilities within the impossible, he reached inside, until the room around him darkened.

"A fool might have doubted you."

Callum recognised Heinrich's smooth voice before his eyes adjusted to the sudden gloom. Little by little, the shape of a man wearing a crisp cream suit defined Frank in the shadows, sitting on the sofa with Jacqueline next to him. Both were unrestrained, their manners awkward as if a stranger they didn't like had invited them for tea. Heinrich slid a firm hand across Callum's chest to announce his whereabouts. Callum pulled away with a scoff.

"A rescue, is it? How mundane." Heinrich looked down at the blood that had stained his clothes when he'd grasped Callum and smiled.

Callum clenched his fists. "There's more where that came from."

"Callum," Frank cautioned him. It was the first time Callum had seen genuine fear in the man's eyes.

As Heinrich kicked the body of the dead commander, Callum realised he was still in the same room. It was darker now, like a shadow of where he'd been before. But every fallen book, destroyed piece of furniture and unconscious Brownshirt lay right where he'd left it. A place that existed in parallel, occupying the same space as the everyday world. The idea might have excited him, were he not so preoccupied with small matters like rescuing Frank and not dying.

"A simple human might try to make good on that threat." Heinrich tutted his tongue as he stepped over the corpse. "Oafish bastards, aren't they? Of course, oafish bastards often come in great numbers. With enough sustained anger, they can level nations. That fury will feed my master for centuries to come."

The images of Heinrich's awful kiss returned from the back of Callum's brain, and their re-emergence tasted like death. Callum felt every bit of it in the pit of his stomach. The pain. The loss. The fear. Over and over, feeding on its own endlessness. For all Heinrich's evil, he wasn't a liar. Each horror dragged through Callum's mind with grim inevitability. There was no longer any question as to whether each image would come to pass, only how long it would last, how many times it would happen, and how many souls it would destroy.

In the depths of his gut, each new death fed him its own strange rapture. He could smell ash, taste blood, feel the fires against his skin, but far from the terror it had raised in him in the Tiergarten, or in those first seconds of its return, each new horror now filled a void and purpose he'd not understood or even noticed until now. Callum stared at his hands as inch by inch, the fleshiness of his palms returned, the living world reclaiming him as Heinrich's master feasted on death. Perhaps, in some cruel, immutable way, he understood the feast they required. A natural, rotting decay. A work, not of monsters, but of men.

"*Callum!*" Frank's voice broke through the fugue like a stray ember that had singed his mind's eye. The effort visibly exhausted the man.

The winds returned, humming just as they had when Callum had pushed his hand so foolishly into the green hole. A dark wind to obscure the truth behind the hellish feast.

"Where is your master?" he asked Heinrich.

"Here, there, and everywhere," the man answered with a playfulness as helpful as it was precise.

Callum felt another familiar sickness in his gut. Was it Max's presence, or had he imagined it? He now understood Max could not occupy his body for long, for fear of destroying them both. Such was his growing familiarity with death and its persistent spectres. But Callum needed Max now. With their combined might, could they take Heinrich down like they had the Nazis? Perhaps with help from Frank and Jacqueline, but even with the combined might of all four—the human, the vampire, the ghost soldier, and whatever Callum was turning into—their fight would not be won with brute force.

Jacqueline's gaze held his, as fearless as it was inquisitive. No more was she simply the catty socialite that kept Robert's company. Far from horrified or helpless, see looked intrigued.

"I mean it," Callum said with a voice as calm and reasoned as the look on Jacqueline's face. "If you expect me to give your master this feast—"

"Give it to Them?" Heinrich laughed. "You overstate your importance."

Callum nodded, keeping his cool. "Whatever They need from me, They can have it. But I want Max. I want the two of us to be together, unbothered and at peace. After that, whatever your master feeds on, whatever this brings into the world or changes, I want no part of it. Not even a glimpse, is that understood?"

"Oh, Callum," whispered Frank, wearily shaking his head.

Heinrich gave Frank a grin that chilled Callum with its false sympathy. "Three times now, you have invoked his name. What are you expecting, friend? What loyalty do you think he owes you? Perhaps you simply fear what is to come. I can take that fear from you, if you wish."

Frank's scream echoed off the room's darkened walls. Ropes that had not been there before now glowed like fire irons across his skin, cutting through his clothes as they tightened.

"Stop it!" Callum threw himself hard against Heinrich, which sent the villain stumbling, even as he laughed. "I've already said I'll do what you want!"

Frank's screams faded to a staccato whimper that didn't make Callum feel much better. For her part, Jacqueline had stayed well clear of the burning ropes, which vanished as quickly as they'd appeared.

"You, Callum, understand better than any of us that there is more to the world than what we see."

"Just tell me what you want."

"Cal…"

Callum tensed, sure that Frank's murmurs would get him a fresh round of lashing burns. Jacqueline had peeled away his ruined clothes, revealing the gruesome scars Heinrich's demonstration of power had left behind. Jacqueline shook her head, her face grim.

"And you'll fix Frank up too, if you want my help."

"Oh, so now you want to bargain?"

"I mean it! And don't tell me you can't do it. This is your bloody handiwork."

Heinrich tilted his head, his face seeming troubled, if only for a second. "Unfortunately, my powers have never included those of healing."

"You miserable bast—"

"Don't worry. When my master arrives, you may petition Them directly." The man's inscrutable expression left Callum unsure if this was an offer or a threat. "But I wouldn't suggest wasting more time."

"Do as he says," added Jacqueline, with no more passion than if she were reading the weather on the wireless. "It's Frank's only chance."

"Only chance?" Callum snapped.

"No," Frank whimpered. "Both of you—"

"It is decided," Heinrich interrupted him with triumph. Without further warning or ceremony, he took Callum's all-but-transparent wrist in an unshakeable grip and guided him toward Frank and Jacqueline. Callum gritted his teeth as Heinrich pushed his hand closer to Frank's raw wounds. If Max was ever going to flex his ghostly powers, now was the time. The monster tightened its grip on him. "Disappoint me now, and I'll see you survive a fate much worse than his."

Callum grimaced as Heinrich pushed his fingers deep into Frank's wound. They pierced muscle and brushed bloodied and blackened flesh as screams filled the room. At last, with Callum's hand good and coated in the slickness of Frank's blood, Heinrich withdrew it and walked Callum with cold deliberateness to the hole behind the mirror. The gateway that had brought him here from the Institute's mortal surface.

Contact with Callum's hand brought forth the swirling green mists as surely as if he'd summoned them himself. They sucked the blood from his hand with an unnatural hunger. The green mists brightened until they became a white light Callum could no longer watch without being blinded. But Heinrich watched with a fascination that gave way first to awe, then to a humility that bordered on joy, something Callum would never have expected to see on the man's face.

Callum leapt away as a long white tendril of energy burst from the hole, widening it until it consumed the wall around. The portal was now big enough for Callum to pass through, should he ever wish to take complete leave of his senses. What had he done? What had he let into the world? He shot a quick glance at Jacqueline, who looked back at him with steady resolve. He'd no way to know the vampire's mind. No way to know what she expected to come next. But the look on her face left him two simple possibilities. Either this would pass like a bad dream, or they would all soon die here, Heinrich included.

"Beautiful!" The zealot gazed upon his deity, unbothered by the light. "Have you ever seen anything so miraculous, Callum? Are you ready for what you most want in the world?"

Callum could barely hear him over the wind that now howled through the opening. Jacqueline laboured to get Frank's arm over her shoulder and began dragging him toward the light. Callum was beside her in a flash, trying to take Frank's weight. "What are you doing?"

"Callum," Frank said in a voice so weak, Callum feared their tussling would finish him off. "Trust her. You're about to be more… more impor…"

Jacqueline shook her head as Frank's lolled to one side. "He won't survive here. Please!"

Callum didn't know what made him believe her. Perhaps it was her cool head amidst this madness. Perhaps it was her ability to stay beneath Heinrich's radar. He was helping to manoeuvre Frank's weight toward the portal before he knew it. They'd barely neared it when one of the tendrils, its energy sharp as a living bolt of lightning, wrapped around the wounded man's wrist and pulled him in.

Heinrich stared in amazement, then let out a cruel laugh. "Make your pleas quickly, Callum. I think my master is hungry."

Callum's stomach tightened with rage. Frank. They'd given up Frank, and for what? To feed Heinrich's god? He lunged at the man, but Jacqueline held him back with surprising strength.

Heinrich fell to his knees, whispering, his voice joining the winds in grim harmony. "Claim this world's undying armies." Heinrich dipped his finger in the congealing blood of the Nazi at his feet and smeared it across his face. He began unbuttoning his shirt, stripping himself to the waist before smearing more blood across his bare chest, down his arms and over his muscular shoulders and neck. More tendrils reached from the doorway, caressing Heinrich's face and body, suckling on him like leeches of energy and light. The man's grin was blissful Nirvana on his face.

Would the being kill him? Callum didn't trust it to stop with Heinrich if it did. But before they could act, the light creature withdrew into the doorway. The rest of the room's light began to fade, until all that remained illuminated was Heinrich's face. The man's eyes grew wide with anticipation, then fear as he watched the portal, licking and biting his lips.

"Your master doesn't like how you taste?" Callum asked.

"Be silent! They…" Heinrich's grimace softened as the gentle green light filled the room, revealing the figures of the Brownshirts, each now up and about, eyes shrouded in the same green mist. Each and every pair of those eyes was on Heinrich.

"You're here," Heinrich whispered, his face full of joy once more. "You've come."

One of the Brownshirts said something to Heinrich so soft and fast, Callum couldn't catch it, much less understand. Then, another spoke, just as inscrutable as the first. He turned to Jacqueline for translation, or at least some clue, but she was nowhere to be found. He was alone in a room with a supernatural cultist and a troop of Nazis possessed by a warmongering god.

Callum watched the Brownshirts draw closer and closer to their servant, until the brush of flesh on his hand made him flinch. Quickly and silently, the hand gripped his, giving him a gentle squeeze before its owner added his own line to the incantation. There was something familiar about that squeeze, and that voice.

As his comrades circled Heinrich in their newly borrowed bodies, Max remained at Callum's side, Heinrich safely distracted from either of them as the ghosts knelt to entertain the man's delusion. Callum clutched Max's hand tightly as Ferdi and the others caressed Heinrich's face, throat and chest, his muscular arms and shoulders, laying him down on the floor, where he surrendered fully to the god that had not come.

Ferdi was right. For them, there would be no more gods. No more masters.

Max held Callum close as faint sighs of pleasure filled the darkness. Slowly, they turned, dancing to music neither one could hear. Heinrich's sighs became gasps, then cries, then screams as Max tried to shield Callum's eyes from the ghosts now tearing Heinrich apart. Callum couldn't resist, watching them tear at flesh with their bare hands. But even he had to look away as one brought down a blade to sever Heinrich's foot at the calf, and Heinrich's scream filled the room.

Ernst was a cunt.

Callum didn't dare look back until all was quiet. When he did, he barely recognised the creature that had been Heinrich. With a solemnity that belied their viciousness, the ghosts cast the remains into the doorway like wood on a fire, at last stepping back as the tendrils of light emerged again, tentative as stray cats lured from their hiding place with scraps of fresh meat. One by one, they wrapped themselves lovingly around the ghosts' host bodies, even as one of those bodies lingered back.

"That's our ride home," came Ferdi's warm voice through the smiling, bloodied lips of the bearded man Callum had thrown into the mirror. "Don't keep him long." He didn't pester Callum and Max further, allowing one of the tendrils to grasp him as it had the others.

Callum and Max stared at each other, a fine pair, the disappearing man and the ghost possessing a Nazi. Callum tried to ignore the short, dull haircut, the grizzled, unshaven jaw and the slightly bent nose that looked nothing like Max. Did it matter what Max looked like? Or what Callum looked like… or didn't?

"Come?" Callum took both the man's hands in his and squeezed, until Max drew near enough for their lips to touch, one long kiss completing their sweet illusion, *Fleisch* upon *Fleisch* one last time. Far from the bitter taste of this stranger, the kiss was all Max in its tenderness, and for one fleeting second as he withdrew, the ghost looked like himself.

"Yes," Max said, grinning as the last tendril wrapped itself around his host body. "I know you will come."

Callum watched the thing pull Max's spirit through the doorway, just as it had Ferdi and the others, leaving their mortal shells behind. Their farewell had lasted only a moment, but it was long enough for Callum to promise himself—and Max—that he would return to Berlin, to the bar within Suzi's, where Max would be waiting.

With the last tendril gone, the opening vanished, returning the room to its ordinary state. The winter sun warmed its windows, lighting the bewildered Nazis, who stood covered top to toe in Heinrich's blood. Knowing he was barely visible, Callum watched from the shadows as each man began to burn, then melt within his clothes. Two of the men ran for the front door, screaming as they went. The man whose body Max had borrowed lifted his pistol and ended it quickly, while the others were puddles of charred flesh, bone, and cloth before they could find their weapons. A ghost was not meant to share the body of a mortal man, though as Callum now understood, he was no mortal man.

"Boys leave such a mess." Jacqueline tutted at the remains as she emerged from the shadows.

"Thanks." Callum resisted a sneer. "You were a great help."

"Frank's alive, isn't he?"

"Is he?"

"I believe so." Jacqueline reached into the hole that had started all the trouble, lifted a small metal ball from it and put it in Callum's hand. "Though the next time you see Frank, he won't remember you, and he won't be him."

Callum turned the perfectly smooth orb in his fingers, fearing he'd break it. "You don't mean… he's this?"

"No," Jacqueline smiled. "He will be human. But this will help you find each other. Then, our work can continue."

"You just said he wouldn't remember."

"That's right. Nor will I, and nor will Robert. Memories can be a dangerous thing. Sometimes losing them is the best thing you can do." She gently closed his fingers over the ball. "Robert will be here soon with all the information you need."

"Information?" Callum shook his head. "*Our* work? I'm not a part of this!"

"Then why didn't you go with Max? Disappear into nothing?"

"I…" Callum thought back to his conversation with Heinrich in the snowy Tiergarten. The man had asked what he most desired in the world. But what did he most fear? He looked around at the remains that dotted the room. "We should—"

"Don't worry. The Institute will have to clean up more than this before it moves on. It can't stay in Berlin now, any more than we can. Magnus and Karl have known this for some time."

"I don't give a damn about Magnus and Karl. What are you talking about?"

Jacqueline drew closer to him, at last dropping her imperious airs as she took both his hands. "I know you want explanations. When we're on the train to Brussels—"

"Brussels?"

"Just listen. I can give you some answers there, though the details might be vague by then, and I can't promise you'll be happier for hearing them. You saw what happened here today. Now, imagine what might have happened if Heinrich had succeeded in summoning his master. If I hadn't intervened and led a more benevolent creature to us instead. One that could hide Frank, and carry your spirit friends here."

"For God's sake, enough!" Callum pulled away from her. "You mean there are more of those things? And that that was a *nice* one?"

"I used the word 'benevolent.' I stand by it."

"Nice? Benevolent? It looked hungry to me, and you're telling me you controlled it?"

"I controlled nothing. I just led it here. It's taken me years to master such skills, and when I surrender my memories, it will take more years to get them back. What matters is that you keep the orb safe. Your memories of us will be the only ones intact, so it's imperative that you follow our instructions to the letter. Can you promise me this? *Please,* Callum?"

Callum shook his head. The practicalities landed one after the other on his mind, and none of them made this any easier. For one, how was he supposed to carry anything if he couldn't be seen?

"Thank you," Jacqueline whispered as a car pulled up outside.

"What about Anne?" Perhaps Callum couldn't find it in himself to refuse. But damn it, he would look after Anne.

"She's already on her way to Amsterdam, with Suzi and plenty of money." Jacqueline strode to the front door, admitting Robert.

"I'm none too flush myself," muttered Callum.

"Was that a hint?" Robert asked, gently mocking him. "Relax. When we leave you in Brussels, you'll stay on to Dunkerque and catch the first ferry bound for Folkestone, then a train into London. Your things have been sent ahead to an address in Shoreditch. Our contact will lead you there from the station."

"Lead me? He won't bloody see me!"

"You'll approach him. Look for the word 'Arcadia,' then follow his instructions, precisely. He'll lead you where you need to go. There's also a trust held for you at the Bank of England with all the money you'll need."

"Got all this figured out, have you?"

The pair smiled at him before Jacqueline spoke again. "Fate is a funny thing. Sometimes changeable. Sometimes stubbornly predictable."

"I see. And just how am I supposed to hide this?" Callum asked, holding up the orb. "I can't just wear a suit of clothes looking all empty like, and I'm *not* sticking it up my—"

Jacqueline took hold of his arm again. "Trust Frank, and us, and yourself. Can you do that, at least?"

He didn't know what it was about her touch that made him trust her. But he did, so completely it felt foolish. "Will I see Anne again?"

"You may, if you wish. Though she probably won't see you."

Callum shook his head again, not knowing how to answer, or how he'd get answers. "I suppose that's it then?"

"Except for the small matter of our memories," Jacqueline corrected him. "Ludo jabbed you on his way out, didn't he? I can smell it in your blood."

"Green fingernails? Yes. Bastard might have warned me. What's that got to do with anything?"

Jacqueline turned to Robert. "Ready?"

Before Callum had time to be afraid, the two vampires bit him with kisses so gentle, his entire body felt like it was floating through a dream.

CHAPTER THIRTEEN

"Once we get to Brussels, where do you think you'll go?" Callum asked.

"Hard to say," Robert looked at Jacqueline. "Back to Paris, perhaps?"

"We've done Paris. Time to look forward, don't you think?"

"Spain then? I've been missing your homeland."

Jacqueline winced as if the idea pained her. "And trade one incoming dictator for another?"

"How about yours then?" Callum asked Robert, realising he knew nothing about Robert's origin. "How long since you've been home?"

"Have you spent a winter in Denmark?" Robert shuddered. "Besides, I've long been a proponent of 'home' being wherever I happen to be."

"Fair enough."

"Stockholm?" Jacqueline asked.

"See prior note about the weather and add an obnoxious dose of House of Blood politics. Pass."

"Iceland, then? Little politics there."

"True, or much of anything else. Be sensible."

Callum laughed. "You're running out of options, mate."

Jacqueline regarded him with a mischievous smile, squeezing his hand. "Los Angeles. Let's go."

"Los Angeles?" Robert laughed. "Beaches? Movie stars? Nary a cloud in the sky? You're—"

"Perfectly serious. Why not give it a chance? Lots of us are doing it."

"All the more reason not to. How about New York?"

"Not if you want to avoid politics."

They sat in silence for a moment, letting the question hang in the air.

"Fine. Chicago first," Jacqueline acquiesced at last. "But only for the summer. Then, it's on to California."

Robert frowned, before a smile crossed his face. "How did I mentor someone so insufferably practical?"

"Because it's the sort of companion you need the most."

Callum let the remark pass without comment.

The sound of the compartment door sliding open interrupted them. "*Fahrkarten. Reisepässen.* Tickets. Passports."

Robert handed the documents over, while Jacqueline stroked his arm, playing the dutiful 'wife' to minimise scrutiny.

The attendant punched both tickets, inspecting the passports before handing them back. "Good journ—"

Callum shifted uncomfortably in his seat as the man stared right at him.

"The gentleman said he was going to the restaurant car," Jacqueline explained. "Though he's been gone more than an hour."

The guard muttered something under his breath in German.

"It seems lots of people are leaving Berlin any way they can," Robert added.

The man squared his shoulders, fixing them with a glare. "You do not like our capital?"

Robert looked at Jacqueline before turning back to the guard. "We hope to like it again, some day."

With a brusque nod, the guard was gone.

"When did it happen?" asked Callum, staring through nothingness where his hands should have been.

"A bit before Hanover, I think," Jacqueline answered, not unkindly.

"Thanks for not telling me. I could have gone tomorrow and saved us the ticket."

"He can't have looked too closely," Robert said, pointing to Callum's legs. "You're still making an indent in the seat.

Callum chuckled at that. "Wait, he couldn't see my clothes?"

Jacqueline smiled. "Or the little gift tucked inside them. You'll have to learn to obscure them yourself, soon enough. I'm told it's quite the mental effort. For now, you needn't worry."

The train ride continued in silence before Robert spoke again. "So, where will you go, mystery man? Want to join us in Chicago? Los Angeles?"

"With all those Yanks?" he muttered.

"Ah, yes, probably best you don't. Back to Nottingham, perhaps?"

Callum gazed out the window as factories on the outskirts of Cologne whipped by. The day was clear, and he could just make out the spires of the famous cathedral looming over the darkened city. "I was thinking Australia."

"Australia?" Robert laughed. "You're serious?"

"I think I am."

Jacqueline nodded with approval. "Then perhaps one day we'll see… or rather, meet you there?"

Callum shrugged. "Will you know me, if you do?"

"My memory's not that feeble," boasted Robert, his grin flashing a careless hint of fang.

Callum turned his gaze to Jacqueline, but there was no point in asking. The serum released into Callum's blood had already begun taking Robert's memories, and Jacqueline's would soon follow. Within the hour, or perhaps less, their memories of Callum, Frank's secret cabal of supernatural research, and those last days in Berlin, as well as Max, and a hidden club for the spirits of fallen men who loved men, would be Callum's secrets alone. Jacqueline had already forgotten her promise to share more details on the train, though Callum had all the information he needed. Arcadia. Hardly a word he would soon forget. He allowed himself to fade from his companions' conversation, just as he had their sight, until they stopped looking at him completely. Then, when the train disappeared into the darkness of the next tunnel, he took his leave.

EPILOGUE

The freight ferry journey to Folkestone had been hell on God's dark earth, but Callum had managed to sleep through most of it, evading prying eyes until there, on the platform at London Bridge, he spied a man reading a white book with ARCADIA written across its cover in bold blue letters. The vampires were as good as their word. The trust, the apartment… Callum had no idea what to do with so much money, but it was just one more thing he'd yet to master.

His wealth, combined with his now permanent invisibility offered him remarkable freedom, yet the awkwardness of paying for items as an unseen man had often made petty theft an easier option. Not every day-to-day task could be handled by mail or telephone.

Unlikely assistance arrived one night in the summer of 1934, when an ambitious eighteen-year-old burglar named Alex Harper sprained his ankle attempting to score some fast loot from Callum's 'vacant' apartment. Spooked as he was, the youth was also blessed with an open mind and a vivid imagination, so it had not taken him long to decide that a fair wage in the service of his unseen mark was better than prison time, and after four months of loyal service, Callum invited Alex Harper to stay.

The pair lived, cooked, and ate together, though it had taken Callum some time to get used to eating in front of another person, and Alex some time to get used to watching an unseen person eat. They explored and studied tomes of the supernatural—much easier to source now Callum had a visible colleague—and occasionally thieved together from those who could afford it, just to keep in practice. Another month passed before Callum first felt Alex in his bed, where the young man continued to spend his nights. By the time the pair fled to Dorset to escape the bombs they'd both known would come to London, Callum's was a one-bedroom household once more.

Callum's growing talents kept Alex from the draft, though extending his condition to envelop another person took a physical and mental effort that laid him out for days each time. He couldn't resent it. While memories of Max prevented Alex from entering Callum's heart as easily as he had his flat, the young rogue had given him a family, of sorts, to replace the one he would never see again.

He never even saw Anne again.

One by one, headlines promising peace brought jubilation to the streets. Germany surrenders. Japan surrenders after… Callum read the headlines with horror, remembering all that Heinrich had shown him. The camps. The bombs. Images filled with death. They'd stopped it though, or stopped it from getting worse, at least, or from lasting forever. Hadn't they?

Yes. Together with Max and the others, he *had* stopped things from being much, much worse.

Another headline late in the year promised passage to Australia from Tilbury for just ten pounds. When Alex wouldn't take 'no' for an answer, Callum knew he was out of excuses. They shared a good laugh at the irony of two petty thieves voluntarily emigrating to Australia, then spent the rest of the morning making love.

Alex Harper died of a lung infection twelve years later at the age of forty-one, having never seen the face of the man he'd loved. Buried in Waverley Cemetery in a modest plot overlooking the sea, he left a sizable estate and a large Paddington home to a trust administered by his 'brother,' one Kelvin Harper. This brother remained quite unseen, and those who made the attempt found no photographs or formal records beyond confirmation that the man existed. With no living family to mount a legal challenge, the property sat empty until the winter of 1981, when neighbours noticed lights on in the house once more. Some speculated the place had been bought by the local diocese as a nun's cloister. Sarah Tucci of 19 Glenmore Road was adamant that she had spoken to a young nun coming out of the place who she described as "the rudest cow who ever ignored someone." Others claimed the house had fallen to more sinister uses, believing they'd heard strange chants or seen unusual lights behind the often-drawn curtains. More outlandish tales of black goats being delivered in the dead of night, or backyard orgies around a bonfire were met with good-natured chuckles which discouraged closer scrutiny.

Kelvin—as he now called himself, for the ruse had stuck—enjoyed having the company of a female friend again, tough as she was. Alex's death had hardened him too, though not so much that he'd failed to recognise that gleam of curiosity in the woman's eye that had once belonged to Frank Bakker.

He thought many times of going back to Berlin. He read about the building of the wall in all the papers, then about *Ossis* killed by Communist bullets for daring to cross it. He sat alone in a darkened cinema, watching Liza Minnelli strut her way around the screen with a devil-may-care bravado that reminded him of Anne. Then, decades later, he sat glued to the television, unseen tears in his eyes as rejoicing Berliners smashed that damned death wall down. What had become of his friends? Had they danced, drank, and celebrated through it all, hidden and shielded within the place that had once been Suzi's? Yes. Once his work with Patricia Bakker was done, and he'd fulfilled his promise to Frank, he'd fulfil his promise to Max and return.

He'd never expected to greet the new millennium. He remained fit, startlingly so for a man of his years. How long could a Cloak Walker expect to live? Some texts claimed a century, some two. How long would Max wait? Would he recognise the cynical bastard his *Geist Flesich* had become?

He watched over Bakker as she befriended and recruited others, including an idealistic young Italian who for reasons he couldn't fathom, believed in Bakker's mission more than Kelvin now did himself. The privilege of youth. In a world of such strange serendipity, how cynical could one old man be?

When he did return to Berlin, he would be as changed as the city was. Changed by Max, changed by Alex, changed by Australia, changed by Bakker… and as sure as he'd vanished from human sight, he acknowledged the one truth he'd felt that day on the platform at London Bridge, spying the stranger with the odd book titled ARCADIA.

He'd only just begun to live.

THE HAUNTED HEARTS SERIES

Curse of the Stag's Eyes – Glenn Quigley

The Night Belongs to Lovers – Ryan Lawrence

Frat Ghost Wingman – Finn Dixon

The Neverloving Dead – Tal Frost

Ritual of the Broken – Seb L. Carter

Shadowing My Dreams – Shane Morton

Medium Rare – J. P. Jackson

Cordelia Manor – Adam J. Ridley

Three Heart Junction – Colin Dereham

ABOUT THE AUTHOR

Christian Baines is an awkward nerd turned slightly less awkward author. Raised on dark humour and powered by New Zealand wine, he is the author of six novels including gay paranormal series *The Arcadia Trust* and *My Cat's Guide to Online Dating*. Born in Australia, he now travels the world whenever possible, living and writing in Toronto, Canada between trips.

ALSO BY CHRISTIAN BAINES

THE ARCADIA TRUST *series:*
The Beast Without
The Orchard of Flesh
Sins of the Son
Tears in Time

Other books:
Puppet Boy
Skin
My Cat's Guide to Online Dating

Praise for Christian Baines

"Baines' underworld is well devised, multi-layered, and dense with political and personal agendas—and it's frightening: so much so that I found myself looking over my shoulder more than once at night." FELICE PICANO, author of *Like People in History*

"Believable characters and rich settings pulled me into this world, and I didn't want to leave it. I was sorry to reach the end." GREG HERREN, author of the *Chanse MacLeod Mysteries* and the *Scotty Bradley Mysteries*

"A wickedly subversive wit." JEFFERY ROUND, author of *The Dan Sharp Mysteries*

"With excellent description and insights into what makes even the most supernatural figures human, Baines will have you staying up late to spend more time in his characters' unravelling world." A.J. DOLMAN, author of *Lost Enough*

"Just fantastic! I just couldn't put it down." SARINA, *Love Bytes Reviews*

"Christian Baines has an incredible talent for writing supernatural beings and making them absolutely credible." MELANIE MARSHALL, *Scattered Thoughts and Rogue Words*

"5 stars! ...a devastatingly good read!" CAMILLE, *Joyfully Jay*

"Christian Baines is a writer with a bold, original vision, a vision not beholden to the limits of conventional genre tropes. This is a writer who knows his own voice, and a writer to watch." MICHAEL ROWE, author of *Enter, Night*

www.ingramcontent.com/pod-product-compliance
Lightning Source LLC
Chambersburg PA
CBHW030142010826
48973CB00002B/678